SAGITTA

BOOK 11 IN THE KINGDOM OF DURUNDAL SERIES

S. E. TURNER

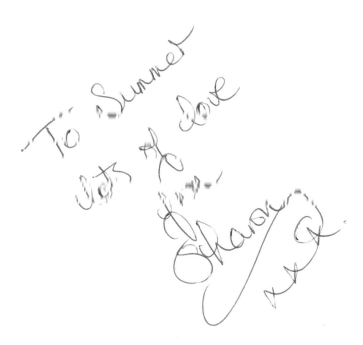

ACKNOWLEDGMENTS

Cover by BookCover Kingdom.
Copy editing by Melanie Underwood
Formatting by Phoenix Book Promo
Beta Reading by Suzanne Pollen
Illustrations by Daisy Jane Turner
My friends and family for their enthusiasm and encouragement.
My three daughters who continue to inspire me.

CHAPTER ONE

The sad little fire gave out more smoke than warmth. A group of hunters gathered around it; one was prodding it to life with a gnarled broken twig, another turned a chunk of meat on a spit. A drop of escaping fat sent the fire into a frenzy and it choked and hissed in retaliation, spitting out its anger. Another hunter coughed and wiped the soot from his eyes, he stretched his bony, knotted fingers above the embers fighting off the chill. He was a thin man, with fine shoulder-length hair that hung in rat's tails around his neck. He pulled a heavy cloak around his body and hunched into a permanent frown.

In the tree above him hung the body of a dragon, blood dripping from its mouth.

The creature was a Sky-Dragon, the smallest of the

winged dragon species. Without the ten-foot wings and the powerful tail, this was no bigger than a mule. They were called Sky-Dragons because of their skill in the air; how they could find the currents and ride them out like a feather. They would rise from the ground and soar towards the sky, hovering for a few minutes until their muscles found the perfect balance, and then would dart away into the clouds. But it was the hovering that made them vulnerable, and the hunter had brought down the Sky-Dragon with a single arrow, dipped in tar and sulphur, which burned the creature from the inside out.

The beast had fallen from the sky, and become entangled in a web of branches. The hunter then climbed the tree and hacked away at the scales, one by one, mercilessly, removing the iridescent blue armour while the dragon was still alive. Another had cut out the tongue to stop it screaming and thrown it to the man below who was building a fire for the meat. As the tongue cooked, the dragon's tears fell silently to the ground, its blood ran in rivulets down the trunk, and its life slowly ebbed away.

Oblivious to the pain and suffering, the hunters had killed many of these dragons over the years, for they believed that the scales gave them strength and power and other mysterious gifts. But the number of dragons was dwindling, and the hunters feared their power was now compromised, though as luck would have it, this dragon was a messenger, and the hunter hacked away at the package it had around its neck. Once on the ground, he searched the contents where he found a map, some parchment and a small jar of ink. Digging deeper he discovered several quills crafted from the dragon's own talons. Opening the map a thin smile curved his lips, for the detail was meticulous. Rendered in dark walnut ink the landscape came to life, the rivers swelled seductively and it smelled of riches, power and wealth. Would he sell this treasure to the highest bidder or would he keep the contents to himself? His heart beat furiously in anticipation as he ran a finger over the dragon palaces and their secret haunts, and as he felt the quiver tremble against his back, he rolled up the map, put it back in its holdall and stuffed it into the jacket beneath his cloak.

CHAPTER TWO

'Did you hear that, Bard?'

The boy leaned forward and then looked round at his mother. He could hear nothing bar the sound of rain and the anxious howls of the night. He was used to those sounds; an animal howling didn't bother him, for he knew they were fodder for his brother.

'I can hear nothing, Mother.'

And it was true, there was no sound of men approaching, no clashing of metal on metal, no yelling and calling out in a tribal tongue. There was no dark magic.

'They will come, Bard, they will come.'

Before, when they had come, Bard would be put in the dragon chambers, where boulders stayed warm from a raging fire far below, and a spring fed water into the hollowed craters in the floor. Dusted with powdery mildew, the chambers smelt of earth and damp, with succulent fungi clinging to walls and colourful alpines clustered in crevasses. Aided by a pair of amber eyes casting a soft glow of light and a plume of fire rimming the enclosure, Bard felt safe and secure and knew nothing of the horrors above.

This used to be a place for the dragonets to mature; for dragons like the heat to grow, and they like the water to shed their infant skin. Their wings grew thicker webbing in there, and the veins spread out like vines over a tree. The colours became richer and deeper, and they stood tall to stretch them out and flex the muscles beneath. Then they moved to the bigger pastures where they roamed freely on the land, lit up the sky with their dazzling colours as the sun baked their skin to the colour of gems, and the water turned their blood-tipped talons to gold again.

Back then, there was nothing to fear from anyone —nothing to fear at all.

Until the hunters came.

Now his brother was bigger, he could not fit in the chamber, and Bard didn't want to go in there on his own. This time, Sagitta had to come out and hide in the caves and Bard had to stand and face the hunters with his mother.

Bard looked upwards, for his mother had shown him the positions of the stars and taught him their names and their constellations within the night sky.

'You see the constellation above us?'

A spot of rain fell like a tear on his face. He nodded.

'That is the constellation of Aquila.'

'Yes, I remember, Mother.'

'Tonight, you must take Sagitta and fly north towards the constellation of Hercules.'

He looked at her aghast and full of terror.

'Once there, you will be safe, for you will have found a place that will protect both you and Sagitta.'

'But I should stay here with you.'

'Bard, it's not safe anymore. There are too many who wish to harm us, too many hunters who want to harm the dragons. You know that I speak the truth. These are the humans who fight wars, who want power and wealth and want to dominate everything around them. They are truly terrible and terrifying with weapons of war that make them stronger and more ferocious than any other species. Be afraid of those humans. Be afraid for the dragons. Sagitta is the last of his kind because all of them have been slaughtered for their scales.'

Bard shuddered. 'Why can't you come with us, then you will be safe as well?'

'I cannot do that. I cannot flee. I must stay here with the sisters and rid the lands of as many of the hunters as I can—so that you and Sagitta will be safe. Once the hunters have gained in numbers there will be little anyone can do.'

'If we all stay, together, then Sagitta can kill all the hunters.'

His mother laughed. 'He is too young, he still has his red scales, you know that. But when they turn green then he will be able to slay anything.'

There was a rumble in the distance. Above him on the ramparts, the sisters beat their shields with their swords and smashed their spear butts into the walls. Their voices rose, thundering into the night, while below them, hidden in the fog, a growl began to rise from the depths. The Mother looked to the east and knew that the faint line of dawn would silver the sky and camouflage their flight path within the next few hours. A sister stood next to her.

'The boy must go now, Zmeitsa. It is not safe anymore. He is the last to go and we cannot take any chances that he and Sagitta will not be slain.'

Zmeitsa creased her brow with concern.

Another mage ranted. 'Why can't they leave us

alone in peace, they have had the lives of so many; our fathers, our mothers, our dragons; their blood and tears still stain our soil.'

'Turning our dragons to balls of fire, then using nets and blades to hack at their skin while they scream in agony, and our people can only stand by and watch.'

They stood and remembered how the murderous arrows had flown towards the dragons and pierced their leather scales. But these were no ordinary arrows forged with metal tips—these were laced with sulphur and tar which ignited the dragons weakest spot, causing unimaginable pain and suffering. When the dragon could support its weight no longer and came crashing down in flames, the hunters rose from their camouflaged positions and surged forward with weighted nets of wire, and the murderous hooks trapped the dragon beneath.

Some died quickly but most did not.

Their screams pierced the night for hours. Their blood turned the dragon world crimson for days.

Zmeitsa threw them a glance. 'Not in front of the boy, sisters, he does not need to know the intricacies and depths that some stoop to for power.'

The sisters went back to their positions and began to chant their magic. Being few in numbers, and without the other dragons for support, they were significantly weakened.

'You must go now, Bard. For deepest magic is about to happen. The sisters are stirring and the undead will rise once more.'

'I can't go, Mother, I must stay here at Castle Dru and fight.'

She looked into his eyes and stroked his hair. 'You are my brave boy, and the only one who can save Sagitta. People are waiting for you as we speak. They will teach you everything you need to know; how to fight the hunters and how to protect the dragons. But more importantly, you are the storyteller who must tell this atrocity to everyone you meet; how the hunters persecuted the dragons of Durundal to virtual extinction.'

Bard wiped away a tear.

The drums started to beat. The chanting began.

'Bard, it is time. Summon the dragon.'

He looked at her for the longest time.

She nodded to him.

Bard emitted a long howl, like a wolf. It was high pitched and ethereal, full of deepest knowledge and links with the creatures of old.

Sagitta heard the call and once out of his cave he launched into the air. In this light, only the nearest trees were visible; beyond them stood the tall shadows and faint lights of the place he called home. As he got nearer he could see the castle against the moonlight, its graceful spires disappearing into the sky. He remembered seeing the other dragons in flight, their shadows linked in a triumphant expanse of wings— now they had all gone; murdered, butchered, maimed, and he cruised the flight path alone. The full moon dominated the sky, pierced by the dark silhouette of the castle's tallest tower and the banner of the solitary red dragon. Candles flickered in darkened windows and fireflies led the way. In the distance a dog barked, it knew that Sagitta was coming. Already something felt different, like a world between worlds waiting for the unexpected and no one knew what the unexpected would be.

Here and there a torch burned on the double curtain wall, casting an eerie glow over the castle inhabitants. The flickering light distorted their faces, making their features appear half-human. The battlements and crenelations were bathed in light as well, as if waiting for some grisly monster to come and take its chances.

The dog barked excitedly as the dragon got closer. It continued as Sagitta flew in from above and looped low, flying into the wind to slow himself. He had done this landing many times and everyone knew to stay out of his way—especially the dog. He opened his wings wide and leaned back. His legs had been tucked neatly against his body and in line with his tail; now he suddenly splayed them out. His hind feet touched the rampart, and his wings flapped furiously to balance as his tail lashed behind him to counterbalance. He flexed his wings once more and showered everyone with droplets of water, then he dropped his front legs down to support his frame. Reptilian eyes were half hidden, and his head lifted on a long powerful neck, his face turned to the distant moon and he opened his magnificent red wings again, freeing them of the rain and spattering the dog in the process. He reared once more onto his hind legs and arched his glistening scarlet neck, straining to his full height. He still had a lot of growing to do, and it was only because he was a juvenile that he was able to balance on the rampart so easily. His eyes locked with the dog's, and then with Bard's.

'He's been enjoying the water, he knows that he has a long journey ahead of him.' Bard stroked the dragon's muzzle when it was lowered.

All of Sagitta's overlapping crimson scales that looked like huge boulders of polished stone were gleaming wet. Bard kissed his muzzle and could feel the heat radiating from his mouth and nostrils while the smell of fire made him feel at ease. Bard scrabbled up the dragon's shoulder, climbed behind his neck, and held on to the tufts of beard that grew wild on his neck.

Zmeitsa stood by the dragon. 'Look after each other now. You are about to go on an incredible adventure and nothing will ever be the same again. But with each other, there is hope—there is always hope.' She kissed the dragon who released a soft plume of smoke, then she kissed the boy's knee, high up on the dragon's body. 'I will join you when I can. I promise.'

She signalled to the dragon and he lurched into motion. Taking off from his elevated position, he fell a couple of feet before his legs and wings engaged, and soon he was soaring high into the clouds, riding the air currents easily, his legs sleekly tight against his body, his wings spread wide.

❧ ❧ ❧

Zmeitsa approached the sisters. 'It is time for us as well.'

'Did you tell him?'

'Tell him what?'

'That you will be leading the assault this time.'

'Now how could I tell him that, Lyra? He is a fifteen-year-old boy who needs to know that his mother will be safe.'

'He would have asked too many questions,' said Lepus. 'He doesn't even know that we can change into dragons, and that's why we have had to hide him in the past.'

'And the reason why we haven't intervened before,' said Cygnus.

'I couldn't tell him,' said Zmeitsa. 'I had to keep it a secret from him, and you all know that we had to keep the strongest and most powerful to the end. We had to give ourselves the greatest chance.'

'With our secret weapon?' said Vega.

'Yes, it's our only chance now.'

'Maybe you should have told him what will happen though,' said Delphinus.

'About what?'

'The prophecy about what would happen if you died.'

'Well I don't intend on dying anytime soon, so I didn't feel the need.'

'And I don't intend on dying either,' said Lepus. 'My secret weapon is at the right levels now. The timing is perfect.'

'Yes, it is. The timing is right to finish this once and for all.' Zmeitsa fuelled them with confidence.

There were howls in the distance.

The sisters looked at each other.

'They are getting closer.'

The mist grew denser, the vines shivered in the breeze, there was no sound at all now; the creatures of the forest knew when to hide away.

'Come, sisters. Let us go to war.'

Neither Bard nor Sagitta heard or saw what happened next as the witches turned themselves into dragons and stormed the enemy lines. The screams that followed could be heard for miles as they curdled the air.

Lyra went first and roared out her yellow flames to get the hunters out of their positions. Her wings moved in sporadic and powerful beats and she twisted her body so it made aiming that much more difficult. She dived in and crushed some with her powerful hind feet, then spun around, and with a lash of her tail, knocked down a score of others. She then began to rise on her hind legs and spread her wings before spitting a mist of venom that would engulf them all. Behind her, she saw Lepus, the smallest and youngest of the dragons, and in the pouches behind her jaw were the pockets of poison that she had been cultivating. She had been waiting years for the poison sacs to mature, and now she was ready. Lepus opened her huge snout and heading towards the attackers unleashed the powerful toxin. The spears of sulphur and tar were aimed at her thick hide—but with streamlined agility, she avoided their poisonous darts and swerved this way and that to spray her toxic rain-cloud over the humans below. The mutagen devoured them—instantly; droplets burned into the flesh, stripping skin from bone in seconds, eyes melted in their sockets, and fingernails dangled from threads.

Cygnus looked on transfixed by Lepus' incredible feats and didn't notice the small group of hunters with their bows drawn back. They fired together, and a dozen arrows hissed across the sky and punctured every part of her body. Cygnus screamed in agony. Delphinus was close by and knew Cygnus had to get to water—fast. She emptied the last few drops of acid over the archers and hurried to the river's edge. Cygnus fell to the ground, consumed in fire, the sulphur already eating into her skin. Within minutes her face was unrecognisable, her talons had completely burnt away, her tail was a mere stump that smoked gently, and the rest of her body was charred and twisted beyond any recognition. Delphinus dropped down to spray the life-saving nectar over her friend's body but she had already passed. There was nothing Delphinus could do.

Another scream. It was a lucky cast of the spear. Even the man who'd thrown it gave a wild shout of surprise as Vega shrieked. She felt a hot stab of unbearable pain, and then blood poured from the open wound. She dropped her wings to the wild cheers of men. She was dying and they were applauding the hunter who struck her. Her eyes glazed over and she started to spin from the sky. She lost consciousness as she hurtled to the ground. And as she died on impact, the hunters stood by her broken body, laughing and pointing, drunk on death.

Lepus came round again for she had seen the events from afar and was beside herself with grief. With her mind not focused on the hunters, she was slow to cover the tender flesh beneath her wings. The delayed reaction was her first mistake and an arrow found the soft vulnerable area and quickly brought her down.

Enraged, Zmeitsa waded into the midst of the hunters, slashing with her claws and lashing with her tail, and every roar she emitted carried a wave of the mutagen with it. She did not need to look for the sisters, she could hear them screaming as the weapons of tar and sulphur punctured their beautiful bodies. At first, she was blinded with rage and didn't see the leader standing before her, but she felt the hot bite of an arrow beneath her wing. She roared in pain and limped towards his retreating body as he fired more arrows at her. She was numb with agony, but still she snapped at him, batting intruders out of the way, breaking bones, severing legs and dislocating joints. She picked up some with her huge talons and ripped them in half, all the time in pursuit of the leader, hissing out the last of her acid breath, praying that the last few drops would flay him and dissolve his cells. Soon his body was full of holes as his clothes disintegrated on contact—his would be a slow and agonising death and his remains would turn to liquid and seep into the soil. As she was savouring the image, another arrow came at her, it struck her and sank into her hide. Roaring, she gathered her strength to spit out the last of the venom that would engulf them all. She drew her head back and felt the glands in her throat swell with readiness. Her power was waning, it was now or never. With one final exertion, the torrent was unleashed and like a tornado, she spun around covering everything in her path.

Pain! Deep, tearing, throbbing, needle-sharp, hammer-blunt pain ripping through her body and her mind, twisting deep inside her and slicing at her skin like barbed wire hooks. Zmeitsa wanted to scream, but her vocal cords had burnt away. She was desperate for water and she could hear it dripping all around her, but her charred tongue found nothing in her mouth but blisters and scorched flesh. The pain was too great now. Her energy was spent. She had nothing left. Her life flashed before her as her heartbeat began to drop and she slowly closed her eyes.

CHAPTER THREE

Bard didn't even have to think about what to do. Sagitta responded to their mother's command by leaping for the sky, eyes focused upwards, neck outstretched, and wings working in perfect symmetry. He was making good, strong wing beats, and he wasn't just flying, he was climbing with determination. He was the one in control and the one who had to look out for his brother. He sensed the fear in the small human and doubled his speed. Bard dared to look back over his shoulder and saw the colour of flames rising murderously against the blackness of the sky, a plume of smoke disappearing towards the stars and the shrieks of battle and death caught in a chaotic frenzy. *Should he turn back and help? They needed the dragons to outwit and outmanoeuvre. Only the dragons had*

the strength and power to send the monsters back from whence they came. Sagitta heard Bard's dilemma and told him, *no, their mother had given strict instructions and neither could turn back now.* Bard shook his head and told his brother that he understood. He found his inner strength and focused on the mission ahead.

≈ ≈ ≈

Sagitta was making good headway and surged forward as Bard gripped on. Bard felt Sagitta's deep easy breathing under his legs and the powerful muscles under his hands driving him forward. The turrets disappeared below him and Sagitta caught sight of the star he was named after, which awakened a deep-rooted instinct in him, for he shivered as he headed towards the sphere nicknamed the arrow. Now he was above the low scuttling clouds, the star would guide him in the right direction, for it gave him the strength and determination and the speed that he needed to get his brother as far away as possible. The travellers ventured forwards with the clouds beneath and a blanket of stars above. Sagitta stretched out his wings and let the balance of nature hold him in place; it seemed as if they were gliding along in a dream. To his right, Bard could see the arc of the sun peeping over the horizon trying to feed warmth into the dragon's scales. They would have to wait a few more hours before Sagitta was saturated from the sun's rays. It was serene this high up and the warmth from the dragon's body pumped round his adolescent frame. Occasionally Sagitta would channel the power from deep within his core and a bright beam of fire would open up the expanse into a corridor of light.

🐾 🐾 🐾

The sun had broken through the clouds and a dense mist that had risen from the warming hills was beginning to burn off. Sagitta lifted his head to stare at the distant sun feeding him the power that he needed after such a long flight. It was noticeably much colder this far north, due in part, to the great body of water that they had just crossed; but now the target was finally in sight. From the emerald canopy of the trees that fringed this land, the hundred gleaming spires of the palace emerged.

Sagitta spotted a good landing site. He angled his wings to slow himself, drifting gently down towards a huge pool that sat a short distance from the entrance of the complex. Beautiful in their construction were nine grey steps that led up to a dais—a tabletop rock, a wide flat stone, about twelve feet square with bevelled edges and engravings of suns, moons, stars and other galactic symbols. The sunlight shone through and lit up a throne of white marble, streaked with veins of gold. On either side of the throne stood two large dragons sculpted from stone, with golden eyes and talons, and upon the throne was seated a statue of a young woman. She was completely naked, except for an embellished necklace of a star that lay against her breast. Her long tresses fell to her feet as she looked down into her palms on her lap. In her hands, she held onto an eaglet—small, fragile, vulnerable, but safe within the woman's clasp. Beyond the throne, another nine steps led down to the clearest waters of a spring-fed pool.

Sagitta began the descent and dipped down towards the palace. Lower and lower he went, and the cool breeze and the fresh smell came closer to greet them. He slowed the beat of his wings and Bard held on even tighter. Then the walls of the palace were rushing up at them as Sagitta suddenly beat his wings faster, his feet braced and his talons skidded to a halt in the sand. He lifted his head to look around and took in his first view of Bergen in full daylight. They had landed by a twisted, ancient tree, and fragrant bushes burst with scented flowers. Orange and lemon trees were laden with fruit. Bard slipped off Sagitta's back and ran over to pick a ripe juicy orange and began to peel it at once. Sagitta did not hesitate to submerge himself in the large pool, and from the way the dragon closed his eyes and sank into it, Bard knew that it was comfortably warm. Sagitta opened his wings and let the moving water gently massage them, the aches and pains eased away with the motion. His brother watched as the water lapped over the dragon's back, spilling over his skin and cleaning the debris of a long exhausting flight. Bard noticed a set of steps descending from the far corner of the pool; he also noticed a pile of clothes. A pair of linen trousers, a tunic top, an orange coloured belt, and a pair of black moleskin slippers. *These must be for me, they look like my size*. He held them up against his frame. *Perfect fit*. He walked swiftly to the steps, checked that no one was around, took off his clothes, pulled off his boots, and submerged himself into the water. This is divine, he thought as he sank to the bottom and rose back up again. Sagitta was already swimming up and down and plunging to the depths then back up again, and Bard watched as the water glistened off his scales and turned them into jewels again. The water was indeed warm and Bard leaned back in the pool, wetting his long black hair and scrubbing at his face and arms. It felt so good, he repeated the process until his skin squeaked clean beneath the pads of his fingers. Bard watched his brother playing in the water and smiled with love.

'You need to go and hunt Sagitta. Go and have a big meal. Then come back here. I will wait for you by the ancient tree. I can forage for a while and pick some fruit, and then we will sleep before we explore our new home.'

Sagitta blinked his large reptilian eyes and lumbered out of the pool. He shook a few times like a giant dog, soaking everything within the perimeter, then urged his enormous body to speed again and flapped his wings into flight. Bard followed him out, dried off quickly in the sunshine then climbed into his new apparel. He scurried along the furrows, crouching low as he made his way towards the orchard then paused at the edge of the trees, warmed by the rising heat of the earth, awash in the sweet scent of newly opened blossoms.

He foraged for a little while before returning to his tree and laid out his small collection. He was contemplating his good fortune when he heard a sound. He detected an intruder and knew that Sagitta wouldn't be returning for several hours.

'I see you've found your new clothes, I'm glad they fit you so well.'

Bard looked up at a man; his age was indeterminable, but he had kind eyes and his face was full of knowledge. Wearing a long white robe with a violet cord around the middle, his hands were folded inside long flowing sleeves. He smiled down at Bard.

'I am Ser Alderman, and I am glad you have arrived safely.'

Bard jumped up and extended his hand. 'My name is Bard and I am here with my brother.'

'Yes, we have been plotting your course on our system.'

'Your system?'

'Yes, our system. We have a giant eye called a telescope and we can see any moving object against the background of the stars.'

Bard looked out yonder and smiled. *Sagitta can do that.*

'But this isn't an ordinary eye, and if we have time, I might show you later today.'

Bard looked at him again. 'Thank you, I would like that.'

'I see your dragon has gone to find some food. There is plenty to be had around these parts, so he will never go hungry.' Ser Alderman looked at Bard's small hoard on the ground.

Bard wished he had covered it over with something. He suddenly felt very awkward.

There was a gurgling sound. Bard shot his head round in response.

'That's the pool filling up again. It refills so it keeps clean at a constant temperature. That way, any new guest that we have will always have a clean bath to relax in.' He looked over to the huge pool and frowned. 'We usually have an assortment of brushes and aromatic oils on the side. At least there should be some orange and cinnamon sticks available. Someone has been very forgetful so I must go and see to that at once.'

A smile tugged at the corner of Bard's mouth as he thought of Sagitta's moment of bliss. Ser Alderman seemed perturbed by the lack of luxuries. 'I will leave you now to enjoy your fruit, it's most succulent at this time of year. But when your brother returns just knock on the door by the gate over there and we will let you in. Though be sure to watch the Dragon Dance that will be starting any time soon. It is quite spectacular. Lupus, ridden by Dom, and Noctua, ridden by Alto, perform this on the night of every full moon.'

'Dragon Dance?'

'Yes, it is an ancient ritual where we bless the continued life of the Grandmaster. It's a very special moment.'

Bard looked over in the direction of a monstrous gate fixed into the stone wall surrounding it and nodded in response. He was still looking at the gate when he saw the back of Ser Alderman hurrying away and disappearing into a small postern door at the side. When Bard was sure he was alone again, he tucked into his fruit, and that's when he heard the music for the first time. A beautiful rendition of reeds and wind stopped his munching, and a sonorous gong sounded as two dragons took to the sky. He was mesmerised by the colours that were churned into the atmosphere from huge cylinders operated by the riders: blues and reds and pinks and vermillion which transformed the air into a purple extravaganza. The first notes of the pipe music shivered across the sky, stilling all conversation and merriment from below. Then the dragons began to move, their bodies taking on the characteristics of different kinds of dragons. This was an ancient ritual where they enacted the sacred duties of the Grandmaster who had sworn to protect the land and all its dragons. Bard gasped as the dragon riders made rain fall with silver streamers, changed the flow of rivers with bolts of blue silk, and stilled winds made of sheer muslin. Then, in turn, each dragon twirled and leapt between streamers that fell from the sky, bringing into movement the virtue sworn by the Grandmaster. Next came an incredible feat of balance, control, precision and articulation, which was performed in the perfect mirror image of each dragon. This dance was called Truth, and Bard was entranced with the breathtaking performance; so much so that the feeling he experienced gave him goosebumps and made the hair on the back of his neck stand up on end. At the end of the dance, he could hear shouts and whistles and applause, and that's when he saw Sagitta coming in to land.

CHAPTER FOUR

When Sagitta returned, the sun was directly overhead. A contented smile was perched on his lips and he sank his full belly to the ground. There was nothing he liked better than the sun on his back, a stomach full of food and an hour or two to snooze.

'I'm just off for a little tour of the place,' said Bard.

Sagitta let out a plume of smoke in response.

'So you just stay here and wait for me okay?'

One heavy lid dragged open.

'Okay, I'm going now.'

The dragon stretched his huge head forward and rested it on his front legs—asleep.

Bard looked back a couple of times as he walked slowly up to the postern gate, but Sagitta was already in a deep repose and dead to the world around him. At the threshold, Bard knocked a few times and a young man in a long white robe with an indigo cord around his waist greeted him.

'Good afternoon, Bard, I trust you have managed to get some rest.'

'I have, thank you.'

'I am Fellow135, one of the many Officials that help run this complex. I am here to take you to Ser Alderman.' The young official closed the gate and gestured for Bard to follow him.

'Yes, he is expecting me.'

'Did you have a good journey?'

'I did, thank you.'

The ancient city of Bergen stood intact, just as his mother had explained it. Under the warm midday sun, the towering palace of gold and silver stone gleamed and beckoned. Here, the Officials, in their white robes and appropriately coloured cords, welcomed the dragons and the Tribunes and made sure that every possible need was accounted for.

'You will notice how the Officials are all dressed in the same white robes. Apart from our Grandmaster who wears a purple robe with a gold cord, but as we only see the Grandmaster from a distance, you probably wouldn't notice. For everyone else, it is the colour of the cord that denotes position. So, for example, Ser

Alderman wears a violet cord, I am a Fellow, so I have an indigo cord.' He checked for understanding. 'Would you like me to carry on?'

Bard nodded his head as the Fellow listed the Heralds who wore green cords, the Readers had yellow, the Temple Boys were given red, the Guardians displayed blue, the Sword Master and the Physician wore black and white respectively.

'The Tribunes, which are also known as the recruits, each have their own dragon. You all wear loose white trousers and matching tops with an orange cord. I can see that the ones I left for you are a perfect fit.'

Bard nodded his head. 'Yes they are, thank you.' Then he noticed how the palace interior complemented the scales of the dragons and the cords. 'All these mosaics and vibrant colours, must have taken years of hard labour to complete.'

'Indeed. This place is thousands of years old, we have books and other literature to give us an approximate timescale, but we cannot be accurate other than to say that some of these stones and gems are so very rare, they will probably never be seen again.'

'A bit like the dragons then?'

'Everything in this place is sacred or rare.'

'And special.'

'Indeed.' The Fellow nodded and carried on. 'The postern gate that you came through opens on to one of the many training grounds. This particular training ground is for combat.'

He hurried along with Bard trailing behind him.

'What does a Fellow do?' asked Bard.

Fellow135 paused, turned round and frowned. 'Teach the Tribunes.'

'Everything?'

'There are many of us, and we all have a different discipline, you will learn mine soon enough. Come along.'

'Am I right in assuming your discipline is the sword?'

Fellow135 turned and frowned again. Bard pointed to his pin. 'Your brooch, I noticed it straight away.'

'I shall have to watch out for you. You are very observant.'

'Indeed.' Bard smiled and continued on his journey.

ক ক ক

Stairs led off from one corner of the arena, wound around a pillar and climbed to an upper chamber. There was a main room with a scatter of furniture arranged in a haphazard fashion. The ceiling glowed softly, illuminating the room evenly. A single window looked out over the vast training ground. Bard smiled. Through another door was a dimly lit room with a desk and a chair, of dark wood. This looked out to an inner courtyard of the palace with a temple garden beneath a curved bridge, and gnarled trees over-hanging a pond. The restful energy of the triangle was cleverly directed towards the offices and apartments.

'These offices and apartments are where the Offi-cials reside.'

'Where do the Tribunes go?'

'Ser Alderman will show you to your room later.'

The Fellow took him past a range of different sized apartments until he stopped outside one. 'Here we are, and I know that Ser Alderman is expecting you. I will see you later.'

Bard stood outside and watched Fellow135 scut-tling along the path; he looked back and gestured for Bard to knock on the door.

The kindly face of Ser Alderman answered. 'Bard, you have made it, and welcome to your new home.'

'Thank you.'

'Come in, come in, sit down wherever you would like to.'

A huge reception hall was tiled in marble and in the centre, a massive staircase led up to the first floor and into further rooms of elegance. At the very top, a dome was painted with landscapes of seas, mountains, and meadows. A feeling of flight and supremacy ensued.

Downstairs, off the main hall, was an imposing room of immense character and wealth. The walls were gold, stuccoed with dragons coiled around several ornate niches. Its roof was lapis and curved into an arch where huge nuggets of silver shone out like stars. Several sofas and armchairs were arranged on a plush blue carpet. A tray of tea had been left for the two men. An aroma of apple blossom and jasmine wafted in the air. The eunuch bowed low as Bard came in, and made a backwards exit. The two men took their seats.

'Well, Bard, it is good to meet you at long last,' said Ser Alderman, raising a smile to him. 'We never got much of a chance to chat earlier.'

'No, it was all a bit of a rush, to be honest.'

'A rush? These things are planned for months.'

'Months?' Bard's voice raised an octave, his brows even higher.

'Yes, of course, it is a process that is meticulously planned well in advance.'

'My mother never said anything to me. We were

under attack and she said you would take care of me and Sagitta.'

Ser Alderman laughed. 'I have been trying to get you to come here for many years, but your mother is very stubborn. She didn't want to let you go.'

Bard was nodding his head. 'Yes, I can understand that, she was reluctant to the very end, but with the hunters surrounding us, she didn't have much of an option.'

'Exactly, but you are here now and that is the main thing. Now, before I tell you a bit about this place, how do you like your tea?'

'As it comes. Thank you.' Bard was deep in reverie and tea was the last thing on his mind, but he had been brought up well and would never decline a beverage from the host.

Ser Alderman poured the tea, then added the milk, a cube of honeycomb for sweetness, and the ritual was complete. 'This place is so vast that some label it as a city for scholars, and a vibrant city it is. It was built long ago by the dragons as a place for the finest minds in the kingdoms to gather and study the great mysteries of life. Many visitors have already spent years studying the collections of tomes and scrolls and leather-bound journals housed in the libraries and gone on to spread the word. But, more recently, and with the decline of dragons and intellectuals, it has become a place to protect the dragons and teach young scholars the art of defence.'

'That is really interesting Ser Alderman, but how do you select the scholars if no one comes here by choice?'

'That's a very good question, Bard, and one which I will try to answer as best I can.' Ser Alderman took a few sips of tea, put the cup and saucer on the table, then pressing his fingers together, he leaned back in his chair and sighed loudly.

Bard was perched on the very edge of his chair and leaned forward in anticipation, his tea already finished.

'We have an observational tower which we affectionally call, Titan; it's an enormous round cyclopean building and the largest on the complex. It is four stories tall with sky flung monoliths, where a wealth of information is sent out and received by the Officials, who then decipher every code and set of instructions in minuscule detail.'

Ser Alderman leaned forward and took another sip of tea. Somehow Bard had edged even further off his seat.

'In the very centre of the tower, we have a giant telescope. It runs from the very base of the building at ground level and soars out of the top of the building totalling some three hundred feet. Titan is built on a pocket of electromagnetic energy, and it connects to similar pockets all over the world.'

'Did you make this?'

'No, like everyone else here we were summoned. Titan has its own brain, a brain that is unlike anything we have ever known before. We have studied the literature in the library and the Grandmaster has consulted the Book of Knowledge, but nothing tells us much about Titan's origin.'

'How does it work?'

'Like I said, it used to send out messages to dragons and scholars all over the world, summoning them to learn the mysteries of life. More recently it sends us dragons and Tribunes, who are trained to defend it.'

'How does it do that?'

'Subliminal messages, telekinetic messages, electromagnetic energy, low-frequency energy, dreams, transmitted thought. All the summoned Tribunes have the power to read and transport messages just by thought alone.'

'So every boy here has been summoned?'

'Yes, every boy that is except Dram. But he arrived with a dragon's egg in his possession, so we made the decision without Titan.'

'Are they all from the same place?'

'At the moment, yes. In fact, Davio and Alto, who you saw flying today, are both from Ataxata which is South of Durundal.'

'Yes, I've heard of it.'

'They were both working for the Emperor of Ataxata when they received their calling and made their way here. Dom and Haynes who ride Lupus and Pyxis, are from the East Coast, they worked together as fishermen, and both received their calling in the same way. But come to think of it, Ijja is from the East Coast as well, and we didn't get any data for him; but as he worked alongside the other two, we thought there must have been a mix-up, so he is here as well.' Ser Alderman shrugged his shoulders.

'I wonder what Titan looks for?'

'I don't know, but the data comes through long before they arrive, so we know who everyone is. Except for two that is, Dram and Ijja.'

'How long do they stay?'

'We have said three years in training, then they can stay on as an official, or return home.' 'And most stay on I presume.'

'Yes, I think Ramou is set to leave us soon, but he comes from a privileged background, so he might want to take up his duties there.'

Bard was nodding as he took in all the information. Ser Alderman poured himself another cup of tea. He offered Bard a refill via a raised eyebrow and a nod towards his empty cup. Bard declined with a raise of his hand. Ser Alderman sipped slowly from his teacup and when he had finished, rang a small brass bell. The eunuch appeared promptly, and with a nod and a smile from Ser Alderman, he quickly and efficiently removed the tea tray without a word. Ser Alderman noticed Bard had sat back in his chair now and was looking much more relaxed and at ease. Now was a good time to begin the tour. He leaned forward which grabbed Bard's attention.

'Would you like to look round the complex?'

Bard sighed, a sort of gratified sigh. 'Yes, I would, very much, thank you.'

CHAPTER FIVE

'So how many Officials are there?' Bard continued with his questions as they walked round the grounds.

'To be honest, I don't know the exact numbers, but somewhere around a thousand.'

'Fellow135 told me about the different coloured cords.'

'Yes, the Grandmaster decided on the colours.'

'When will I meet the Grandmaster?'

Ser Alderman stopped abruptly. 'No one sees the Grandmaster. It is forbidden. Only myself and the chosen eunuchs who are assigned to such a high position. And each eunuch has pledged an oath to never divulge what they see.'

Bard gulped so hard, he didn't think he should ask

what would happen to anyone who caught a glimpse of the Grandmaster, so he searched for another question as Ser Alderman resumed the pace.

'What does the Grandmaster do?'

'The Grandmaster found this place. The Grandmaster is the highest being known to mankind and remains hidden for security reasons.'

Bard nodded, 'I see.'

'Let me show you to your room, Bard. It's this way.'

An avenue of halls ringed the outer perimeter of the Imperial Palace. Each hall had been carefully built at the compass position of the star it honoured and was the home to Ser Alderman and his apprentices. Ser Alderman's hall was in the north of the complex and although it was enormous on a grand scale, it wasn't as big or opulent as the Grandmaster's residence. Here, two grey stone statues of dragons guarded the gates, that stood bigger than Sagitta and twice as wide. The one on the right held a compass in its claws, the other one looked up to the constellations. Going past the Grandmaster's residence, a gleaming black pebbled path led to an impressive glass wall. It seemed to move like a slow ripple of water because the stones had been laid in a subtle graduation of matt to polished that caught the rays of the sun. At the end of the path, a waterfall cascaded down a carefully haphazard run of ledges, pooling into a white marble bowl. On either side of the path was a cluster of rocks on flat swirling paths of black and white pebbles, and an intricate weaving of waterfalls, streams and pools emitted a muted burble of flowing water.

To the right of this feature was another huge building with an entrance that opened from two stable doors. Here, were the baths; steaming vats of hot water where the Officials and the dragons would take refuge from bad weather. The dragons, in particular, soaked their skin in copper baths of luxurious oils that kept their scales smooth and hardened their claws. Next to the baths were the dragon pens and next to those were the Tribunes' rooms. Ser Alderman opened one of the doors and Bard stepped over the threshold.

The room was fairly standard: a beechwood floor and a dark wood table surrounded by four sturdy chairs. A long settle was pushed up against one wall with scattered cushions atop. There were two matching alcoves in the back wall, each one displaying a painted scroll. A long bureau of matching dark wood stood against the far wall with a single vase holding an arrangement of lavender. It was a place of quiet serenity. Bard walked over to the left alcove, drawn to the vividly coloured scroll. It was a painting of a red dragon, the swishing tale and uplifted front claws in a swirling sea of tempestuous waves was quite breathtaking. The other was a green dragon, its snout curled back in a vicious snarl, exposing serrated teeth and breathing fire. It was up on its hind legs and ready to attack.

'They are beautiful, aren't they,' said Ser Alderman. 'I have always admired them.' 'They are amazing,' said Bard. 'So lifelike.'

'Everything here will be different to what you have been used to.'

'I can see that already. It's like an artist's palette has been thrown over the entire complex and all the beautiful colours have been released.'

Ser Alderman laughed. 'Yes, I can see why you would think that.'

The room had been dark, but it illuminated as they entered, the candles coming to life and creating a warm glow instantly. There was no hearth for a fire.

'The rooms stay comfortably warm when the temperature drops, but cool when the temperature rises. We don't know how it happens, but we think it is connected to Titan and the electromagnetic forces beneath it.'

'Anything else?' asked Bard.

'The rooms always have a sweet aroma, of apple

blossom and jasmine. Clothes and fabrics always smell fresh. Plants and flowers are in abundance. We don't understand it, but we embrace our good fortune.' Ser Alderman guided Bard through an adjacent door. 'And this is where you will sleep.'

Bard noticed the room was quite spartan with a single bed along one side, a table next to it and a full-length mirror against the far wall.

'This is perfect.'

'There is a small bath in the next room, but you can use the big copper baths in the Dragon House, and of course, you are permitted to use the outdoor pool whenever you wish.'

'It's grand, it's really grand. Thank you.'

'You will notice that you have a panoramic view from all the windows; the sea is to the south, the mountain range is to the north, the forest and dragon pool is to the east, and Titan can be seen to the west. Beyond that are the pastures and hunting grounds for the dragons.' He nodded contentedly as he watched Bard's face light up in wonder. 'I would like to recommend an early start on occasions, for it is a most wonderful experience to witness the sunrise from these high elevations.'

'I will be sure to do that, and thank you again.'

'You are most welcome, Bard, now, let us continue

with the rest of the tour. You will notice that the palace is full of ancient artefacts and memories of the past and it is easy to let your mind drift to an ancient time. We embrace that connection, for then we hope to learn from those connections. And as we learn, we grow.'

'I understand.'

They went down the hall and ventured down the spiralling stairs. Back and forth the Alderman led him, showing him where the official's quarters were, the armoury, the washing facilities, where to get clean clothes, where to put soiled clothes.

Bard was beginning to get the sense of how to navigate round the complex, and once he had got over the size and scale and luxury of the place, it wasn't any different than finding his way around Castle Dru in Durundal. Of course, it had seemed like a maze at first, but now he realised that the dragon pens were at one end of the complex and the landing court was right in the middle. Everything else veered off from the quadrangle and somehow led back to the council rooms and apartments.

Ser Alderman saved the observation tower till the very end of the tour and his pride was evident as they entered the cyclopean structure on the first floor. For inside, the circular tower was even more splendid than outside, with wonderful, brilliantly coloured wall paintings of dragons and chariots, and detailed constellations adorning the walls. Carved pillars circled a giant, wide-girthed monolith, which came from the depths and soared upwards and out of the dome. Brilliant torches in sconces branched out from the ceiling above and shone down on the immense workstations where Officials and Stewards processed the data.

Bard followed Ser Alderman up the stairs to the top level where a number of telescopes were scattered around the perimeter. He was informed how these telescopes were divided into groups depending on purpose; airborne, ground, and stratosphere; then there were sub-groups that collected data for distance, speed and time. Some of these instruments were as big as missiles, others were elegantly long and sleek. Alongside, were sophisticated interferometers to limit the interference and possible miscalculations of background noises. On the second and third floors he was shown the radar systems and telecommunication portals where a group of highly trained individuals manned the stations throughout the day and night.

As Bard was gazing in all directions, he brushed past a table and nearly sent the contents flying— He stopped moving instantly and held on to the table.

Two Officials immediately rushed over to help. 'This is a collection of very rare optical devices with an assortment of lenses and mirrors that collect data relative to proportion and scale,' said one of them.

'I'm sorry, I am just a bit overwhelmed.'

Bard felt a hundred pairs of eyes on him and not one breath was taken as the spinning objects rotated to a nerve-wracking standstill.

Ser Alderman nodded when all was in place again, and the Officials returned to their stations. 'I have one more room to show you, it's on the lower floor.'

Bard smiled sheepishly to the observing Officials and almost tiptoed towards the stairwell keeping his arms pressed firmly against his side. He followed Ser Alderman down the winding staircase to a vast cavernous room on the ground floor which protected the mighty monolith. It came up through the floor like a giant, surging through all the levels and out of the roof towards the clouds above. It took his breath away, for never before had he seen something of such stature, such power, such magnitude. He felt the monolith vibrating beneath his feet and heard the beating heart from deep within its core. 'This is incredible.' His mouth fell open as he followed its journey upwards.

'This is Titan,' said Ser Alderman. 'The master

machine and hub of all knowledge. The most incredible structure known to man, and no one knows its origin. All we know is that it is connected to other giant structures all over the world, and each one has a master plan.'

CHAPTER SIX

After Bard had been shown around the structure and had a look through the many telescopes as promised, they began to make their way back to the beginning again. Ser Alderman was still vocal with information.

'Your dragon is allowed to come and go as he pleases. No dragon is held here against their will. They are free beasts. We do not keep them in cages or locked in at night. I know that Sagitta is used to his freedom, and will feed when he wants, he will spread his wings and fly when he wants, he will bathe when he wants. All that will continue. Our dragons are given the best care, and to encourage a good working relationship with the allocated tribune, each dragon will be mentally fit as well as physically. I know this has been your practice for many years, but I needed you to be aware that nothing will change. I can promise you that.'

Bard nodded his head in understanding as Ser Alderman continued to fill him in on procedures. 'As you already know, the dragons like to eat at first light, and you already know how much a dragon needs to eat; he'll be starving as soon as he's awake.' He checked for understanding. 'There are many feeding grounds for our dragons and lots of rivers for them to drink from. They will never go without.'

They continued the tour as Ser Alderman held his hands out to two ancient buildings. 'Here is where you eat, and here is where you will pay respects for your good fortune. And do you know why the refectory is in close proximity to the Temple of the Dragon?'

'So we can give thanks for our food and our accommodation before and after we eat?'

Ser Alderman nodded. 'Good, good. And be aware that breakfast, lunch and dinner are signalled by a gong. You will begin to understand the different calls in no time.'

Bard smiled in response. 'I know I will, I am a quick learner.'

'I'm sure you are. That's why Titan summoned you. But look there is a practice session going on right now. Let's go and see what they are up to.'

୬ ୬ ୬

The aerial practice grounds were situated far away outside the complex, and several dragons and riders were on the ground watching those that were in the air. Bard scanned the area and noticed all the different coloured cords on the observers. He followed their gaze and saw two riders competing.

'Who are they?'

'The one on the left is Ijja and the one on the right is Saul. Two very experienced riders but I am monitoring one of them, so I need to watch carefully.'

Ser Alderman hadn't taken his eyes off the events from when they entered the enclosure. 'The practice session is very controlled, it is a discipline between dragon and rider, spotting possible attacks and acting upon them, it isn't supposed to be combat, it's much more than that, so observe carefully.'

'The gift of foresight and intuition.'

Ser Alderman took his eyes off the riders for the first time and looked straight at Bard. 'Exactly.'

Around the perimeter the Guardians were stationed with a range of implements to hand; the evidence of previous distractions was scattered on the ground. A nod went from one Guardian to another and within seconds there was a thrum as a dozen arrows were let loose. Both riders saw the impending danger and took their dragons higher. Then a shot of steam billowed from the rafters above, temporarily blinding both dragons and riders. Orders came from both riders to go higher and avoid the steam, but a canopy above opened with a deluge of rainwater.

'This takes a lot of control, Bard. Look how the rider is reassuring his dragon and checking on the other rider as well.'

'The dragons must have total trust in the Tribunes?'

'Exactly, Bard, exactly, and that is why we have practice sessions.'

As the dragons swooped and soared a flock of pigeons was released. They stormed the air and broke the intense concentration. Ijja's dragon suddenly reared up screaming. Ijja gripped on tightly and got her back on the flight path with a sharp yank of the reins and a set of expletives so loud, all the spectators heard every word from the ground below. The dragon swung her head from side to side, swiping in distress at the pigeons that were now bombing her. The other dragon came in to pacify her, but blinded in terror she rammed into him and took the wind out of him. Ijja pulled on the reins again, to which she responded with another rear and slammed into the male knocking his rider from his seat. As Bard's heart missed several beats he told Sagitta to get into position as there would be a dreadful accident if he didn't get here fast. He held his composure and gave the coordinates and position as the rider plummeted to the ground. His limbs were flailing, nothing but stark fear coming from his mouth. Everyone else was frozen to the spot, for there was nothing anyone could do, and if they could, they couldn't act quickly enough.

Then a flash of red bolted across the sky, and with it came the sound of dragon wings amid a rush of air and Sagitta swept down low to scoop up the rider before he hit the ground.

Ser Alderman looked at Bard and shook his head in amazement. 'That, my boy, is exactly what we are training our recruits to do—you have just used your arcane abilities.'

As Sagitta crouched down to let Saul off his back, the stretcher-bearers ran up to take the confused and disorientated tribune away to the infirmary for a full check-up. A Guardian had hold of his dragon and was taking him to the pens for a rub down.

'Follow the Guardian, Bard. I need to speak to Ijja and Saul about what just happened.' He patted Bard on the back, and Bard took Sagitta in the other direction.

CHAPTER SEVEN

There were ten pens in total, huge great things they were, each one at least the size of the grand hall in Castle Dru. With five on the left and five on the right, Bard went slowly down the aisle, observing the names of Tribunes and dragons, cast in bronze and scribed in gold leaf: Pavo, ridden by Davio was opposite Noctua, ridden by Alto. Antares, ridden by Sli was opposite Pardalis, ridden by Saul. Pyxis, ridden by Haynes was opposite Lupus, ridden by Dom. Mensa, ridden by Ramou was opposite Lacerta, ridden by Dram, and Bellatrix, ridden by Ijja was opposite Sagitta, ridden by Bard.

Once inside the assigned pen, Bard saw a bucket of sand for scrubbing and a pail of cold water: FOR CLEANING EQUIPMENT ONLY! written on the side. Though why anyone would want to put cold water on a dragon he didn't know—for anyone who knew anything about dragons knew they hated the cold. He took a handful of sand and polished Sagitta's hide with it. Sagitta loved it, leaning into the grit like a cat being scratched under the chin. The sand polished off dirt and anything else that had got stuck to the scales and was particularly good at cleaning the hide of wings. Sagitta's wings had many peculiar folds and planes, layers of skin and flexible tendons, and thin, flat bones that were almost as flexible as the planes and the tendons. Sagitta wasn't scaled everywhere; the wing webbings were made of tough, thin skin. This type of tough membrane was also around the eyes and nostrils and in the joints. All of the skin needed oiling after the sanding process. The oil soaked in quickly, leaving the hide softer and more flexible and not one grain of sand stuck to the surface afterwards.

Afterwards, the dragons were much more even-tempered and obliging with each other, and Sagitta loved it, savouring every bit of attention, and even helping Bard to those hard to reach spots, by crouching down low or lifting a limb for easier accessibility. He loved keeping himself clean in a huge expanse of water, but particularly enjoyed the scrubbing and exfoliating of old skin. While Bard worked hard at grooming Sagitta, the other riders brought in their dragons and began their grooming regimes. Sagitta was still fairly young and retained the red colouring he'd been born with; he wouldn't turn green till he was fully grown, but there were patches of mottled viridescent already appearing over his wings.

The relaxed and sombre ambience was suddenly broken when Ijja brought his dragon in on a tight chain. The dragon had a heavy collar around its neck and a strong chain attached to the collar. The smallest pull on the chain would close the collar around the dragon's throat making it difficult for her to breathe. She was snarling and foaming from the mouth. The more she snarled, the more the boy tightened her chain, and the collar closed around her windpipe. The sound that came from inside her throat was unbearable, and Sagitta looked up from his induced state of calm. He clocked eyes on the young boy and Bard felt him tremble.

It's okay, Sagitta, Ijja has just got a feisty one to control. Saul nearly died because of her.

It was the boy's fault, he was panicking her. I could feel it.

No, I saw everything, Sagitta, she was spooked by the pigeons.

He did it deliberately, came the response. *He enjoys hurting her.*

Don't be silly, said Bard. *She needs to know who's the boss, otherwise, things would get out of control and more people would get hurt.*

She is terrified of him. He is dangerous and a liability.

Bard looked over and was met with a hostile glare. 'What are you staring at?'

'I'm just checking that you are okay, it was quite a terrifying moment back there.'

'Well, you are just fine because you own the hero of the day. I've been saddled with this pathetic excuse of a dragon who's terrified of her own shadow.' He yanked at the collar again.

'I've known Sagitta all my life, it's a bond we have. Perhaps you should let her know she can trust you, then she will respond more favourably.'

'Look, mate, you might be trying to help, but it's coming across that you are trying to tell me what to do, and I don't take too kindly to that. I thank you for your intervention on the practice ground, but in here you're just another recruit, so if you don't mind I need to teach this reptile a lesson.'

Ijja dragged the poor creature into the stall, yanked her inside and slammed the pen shut so he could begin his punishment. It was difficult to determine what was going on. The sound of water being thrown was evident, the crack of a whip across her skin was also unmistakable. But not once did the creature retaliate. Even though she could sever him in half with her enormous snout and huge spiked teeth, she took the punishment without a murmur. Perhaps she should have flicked her tail in his direction or raked his arm with an extended talon; it would have been easy and would have made him stop. But perhaps it would have made him worse, so rather than take any chances, she kept quiet and held back the screams that were raging inside her.

Bard felt terrible and looked over to the Guardian. He was too engrossed in rubbing down Pardalis, to say anything. *Maybe you are right, Sagitta, she is terrified of him. But if the Guardian isn't doing anything, then we can't. It's not our place.*

Sagitta didn't respond, which told Bard that he thought otherwise. Another freezing pail of water followed another whipping. Bard felt Sagitta tremble again. Was he feeling her pain?

Yes, came the answer. *I feel her pain and her anguish.*

Come, let me finish grooming you, Sagitta, I know how it relaxes you.

But Sagitta couldn't relax; not now he knew the truth.

❧ ❧ ❧

The gong sounded for dinner and Bard felt his stomach growl and followed his nose to the refectory. It was then that he realised how vast the palace was. The sun was just setting, and torches were being lit, and all along the pathways and enclosures, a dim ambience was cast. A group of older boys were just going in and stood back to wait for him.

'Good work today, young man, that dragon of yours is a hero.'

'Why thank you. My name is Bard, I have only just arrived.'

'I am Ramou, this is Sli and this is Davio. Thank the gods you did arrive today. You must be Saul's lucky charm.'

'Is Saul okay?'

'He's fine, just a bit shaken up.'

Ijja skulked past.

'What's that blood on your hands, Ijja?'

Ijja looked at the spots that he had missed and wiped them on his trousers.

'Dragon's blood or yours?'

'Mind your own business, or it will be your blood I'm wiping off as well.'

Sli curled his fist into a punch.

'Leave it,' said Ramou.

'Have you seen the way he treats that dragon?'

'The Guardians have it under control.'

'Have they though? They don't seem to be doing much to help her.'

'How long has he been like it?' asked Bard.

'Too long, and no one does anything about it.'

Bard's questions were muted as the gong sounded again, which indicated the doors would be closing in three minutes. The group found somewhere to sit and took their seats as two lines of eunuchs carrying covered platters filed into the room and positioned themselves along the front of the tables. The eunuch in front of Bard placed two dishes on the table, his eyes downcast. The Herald thumped his staff against the floor and, as one, the servers lifted the silver domes. All along the table were plates full of exquisitely presented food: shredded pork, cabbage tossed with nuts, duck with beans, cold eggs, pickled vegetables, greens dressed in oils, sticky rice rolled in seaweed, cold roasted chicken, smoked flaked fish, and round peacakes served with ginger. Bard didn't hesitate and tucked in straight away.

'So where are you all from? How long have you been here?' he began between mouthfuls of food.

'Most of us have been here about two years now.

We've all come up from the south. I'm Sli from Sturt Manor. Saul and Ramou have been here the longest, three years, I believe.' Sli looked down the table for Ramou.

'Yes,' said Ramou, wiping the gravy from his mouth with the back of his hand. 'I originally come from Condor Vale; my father thought it would toughen me up coming here. Saul comes from a small place somewhere along the River Dru.'

'I'm from Castle Dru in Durundal,' said Bard. 'Not too far from Saul's location.'

'Dram is from Aiden Hall, coming up for three years as well. I believe there was a misunderstanding concerning his departure from there, but he is a nice enough chap, so it must have been something out of nothing. Haynes and Dom over there are from the East Coast, along with Ijja; and Alto and Davio are from Ataxata,' Sli continued.

'Saul is moving up to be an official, and after today, I would think that will be sooner rather than later.' Ramou raised his eyebrows as he scanned the group.

'How does that work?' asked Bard curiously.

'After three years of learning you can decide whether to go back home with your newly acquired skills, or you can take a position here. It is decided by the council of course.'

'Pardalis is getting a bit old as well, so he will be retired soon,' said Davio.

The group nodded and murmured their agreement.

'To Saul and Pardalis!'

The boys clinked glasses and hoped that both of them were making good progress after the accident.

'And Ramou? What will you do?'

'I'm not sure,' said Ramou. 'I do have a good position at Condor Vale. My father is a Grand Duke.'

'Whoooohooooo,' echoed the group together. But it was all in good fun, almost half of them came from privileged backgrounds.

Ramou smiled at his friends.

'And the dragons,' said Bard. 'Do they all belong to you?'

'No, we have been allocated a dragon. But we all feel so sorry for Bellatrix, she really did get the short straw with Ijja.'

'Shhh,' said Davio curtly. 'We can't interfere, it's the Guardians' responsibility.'

They all nodded sheepishly and searched out the Guardians dotted around the refectory.

'So what's your story, Bard? How come you are here?'

'Well, as you know I am from Castle Dru in Durundal. I flew in this morning on Sagitta.'

'Straight into the action then?' Davio raised his brows spooning more shredded pork into his mouth.

'It would seem that way, but I'm fairly confident there will be more to follow and sooner than you think.'

'Why do you say that?' said Sli, his interest suddenly piqued.

'The hunters are close, very close. They have been wiping out the dragons for many years and moving further north. My home is under the constellation of Aquila, and that's where they were last night. My family stayed behind to fight back. I still have no idea how many survived because the hunters are getting more devious. My mother ordered me to come here to learn new skills and gather a bigger force to eradicate the hunters forever.'

'Well, you've come to the right place. This is military training like no other.'

The group of boys laughed out loud.

'This is serious stuff though,' interjected Ramou. 'Very serious. Our training will be stepped up now. You watch, no rest days from now on. All hands on deck.' His face was grim as he searched for agreement from the group. The laughing stopped, but Ramou was keen to build a rapport with Bard.

'Tell us about Sagitta? Where is he from?'

'He is mine. He has always been mine. We have a special bond.'

'I can see that,' said Sli with his spoon poised at his lips. 'It's good to see that sort of brotherhood. We could all learn a thing or two from you.'

They all looked at Ijja. Sitting on his own. And they all knew that whatever demons he was carrying on his shoulders, no one needed to learn more about life than him.'

'Have you been told about the Grandmaster?'

'Only that no one sees the Grandmaster.'

The boys looked at each other sheepishly.

'What? What do you know that I don't?'

'Nothing.' Ramou disappeared into his plate.

'We all think the Grandmaster is a cardinal dragon —a superior being with human characteristics, or even part-man part-beast, but whatever the Grandmaster is, the veil and cloak cover every single part of its body, and no one is permitted to get close.'

'Ser Alderman was very clear about that,' said Bard.

'The eunuchs must see it.'

'But they are mute as well as castrated,' came a whisper from Davio.

'And if they told anyone what they have seen, then it's…' Sli pretended to cut his throat with a knife.

The boys hunched over their food and changed the subject quickly.

ટ⩩ ટ⩩ ટ⩩

The evening went far too quickly, and just when Bard thought he could not possibly eat another morsel, a eunuch put another domed dish in front of him. Honeyed oatcakes. The succulent aroma rose to his nostrils and found his sweet spot and he tucked in as if he hadn't eaten in days. Finally, feeling as stuffed as a well-fed dragon, he thanked everyone for a marvellous evening, which they all agreed it was, pushed himself up from the table and staggered out of the room to finally rest his head on the pallet next to Sagitta. But he couldn't find him. He wasn't there. Though he sensed he wasn't far away. He felt his sadness. He felt his emotion. He followed the sensory messages to the end of the pens and that's where he found him; curled up in a protective embrace around a very bloodied and very bruised female dragon called Bellatrix.

CHAPTER EIGHT

Bard had no source of light in the pen, but the moonlight cast a glow as it crept through the many nooks
and crannies to expose the creatures of the night.
Rustling and the sound of footsteps alerted him out of
his semi-dreamlike state, and rising from the shadows
to see who was approaching at this late hour, he was
greeted by Tribune Dram.

'So you are bidding goodnight to your charge as
well.'

Bard dipped his head and smiled. 'Yes, it's something I have done every day since I was very young. I
can't sleep unless I have said goodnight to him.'

'That's where we are similar then,' said Dram.

'Oh, and why is that?' Bard tried to stifle the
yawn.

'Because I hatched Lacerta myself and have also done this since the day he was born.'

Bard felt his mouth falling open. 'Really? How?'

Dram grinned, keen to share his story. 'I was given a dragon egg by a stranger. This stranger told me to bring him here because I would be taught how to care for him, and in turn, Lacerta would recognise me as his master. So I knocked on the gate, told Ser Alderman that I had been given a dragon's egg, and after inviting me in, he told me what to do. I buried the egg in the warm sand of one of the sand pails and turned it three times a day. I talked to him almost every hour on the hour because I read that dragons are more likely to respond to the person who talks to them while they are still embryos.'

A look of uncertainty spread across Bard's face. 'But I thought you had only been here for three years.'

'That's true.'

'But Lacerta is huge.'

'That's because he is a Mountain Dragon.'

The darkness made Bard feel bold, and he blurted out the question before he had thought it through. 'Someone told me that you needed to leave Aiden Hall quickly.'

The memories came flooding back, and Dram stared at the darkness as he remembered. 'Yes, that is correct, I did. Of course, it was a misunderstanding. The young woman involved accused me of violating her, which, of course, I did not. But my father, answering to the lord of the manor, couldn't have his reputation tarnished, so he told me to pack my belongings and forced me to leave.'

Bard sighed in the darkness and asked another question. 'How did you end up here in the first place, it's a long way from Aiden Hall, especially on foot?'

'I know, I remember it well.' Dram raised his eyebrows as his mouth curved into a smile. 'One slow year rolled into the next. I found work by offering my services during the seasons: planting, growing, harvesting, helping in the winter, helping after the floods; there is always plenty of work for a farmhand. But there was always this pull further north, so I found myself a boat, followed the constellations, and I have filled you in on the rest.'

Bard nodded, feeling sympathetic to his plight and the way that he had been mistreated. He was glad that Dram had nurtured Lacerta, and now had someone who would look out for him. 'It appears it was your destiny, and that's why Titan summoned you here. It's good to meet someone who has a lifelong connection with their dragon.'

Dram nodded his head as he responded. 'It's good

to meet you too, Bard. I also think it was my destiny, and I go to the temple every day to give thanks to the great dragons of old. Lacerta is my best friend. I know what he is thinking, just as he knows what I am thinking, and I know he would give his life for me.'

Bard nodded his head in agreement. 'I feel the same way about Sagitta, it's a very special bond, but tell me, were all the other dragons hatchlings?'

'I know that Mensa is the mother of Bellatrix and Pyxis, so the two sisters would have been raised here. She is the biggest dragon by a long way, so she is definitely an adult mountain dragon, her name means table mountain, and it takes someone as accomplished and proficient as Ramou to handle her.'

'How did she get here?'

'The Guardians say that the Grandmaster found her injured and brought her in. That's when the sanctuary was founded. Pardalis is the oldest dragon, he was also found wandering outside and taken in. Sometimes dragons know they are going to die and take themselves off somewhere isolated. The Guardians believe that is what happened to Pardalis. They say he is an ancient dragon, so his age is undeterminable, but Saul will be changing his colours for an official's role, so Pardalis will be put out to pasture and rested.'

'And the others?'

'Some would have sought sanctuary here as adults and elders. Some mothers abandon their eggs, and that could have happened as well. If the mother thought her eggs would be found and looked after, then they would have made that decision.'

'You know so much about them.'

'I have made it my business to. There are many books in the library if you care to look through them.'

'I will do that, Dram, thank you so much.'

'I will say goodnight to Lacerta now, then I am off to bed; the dragons will go off to hunt first thing in the morning, so I will probably see you then.'

Bard bid him goodnight then staggered off to his room and left Dram chatting to Lacerta.

🐉 🐉 🐉

He lay there for the longest time thinking about his other home, his other life that seemed so far away now.

Castle Dru covered a hundred times as much ground as the Dragon Palace, with outbuildings so large they could hold an entire community. The pens once held one hundred dragons, its food stores were part of an underground maze, and its twelve towers reached up high into the clouds, a jumble of stairs and corridors going on for miles. But the most cavernous room of all was the Great Hall—with its tapestried walls, ornate ceilings, huge hearths, carved oak doors, and pillared surrounds with endless steps up to the royal dais, and to a small child, it looked like everything had been built for the dragons.

He remembered how the Great Hall had been alive with celebrations on his birthday, and that it was the most celebrated day of the year. If he tried hard enough he could conjure up the noise, colour and smells that surrounded him on those special days. His mother would instruct the sisters to become musicians, jugglers, and acrobats on that day; to fly the high trapeze and dazzle the spectators below with their fantastic feats on dangerously high swings. Colourful puppets and masterful illusionists would mesmerise him with their skilful displays and magic tricks—these would usually be part of the extended families that resided in the castle. The most exquisite dishes would be served: peppered trout and roasted chestnuts, slow-cooked salmon and blueberries, spit-roast pheasant and cranberries, sweet pies, tarts and cakes served on hand engraved silver platters, and all washed down with the finest wines in solid silver chalices. There would be banners and flags hanging from the intricately carved oak supports, displaying the Durundal coat of arms, and thousands of lanterns positioned on the slender marble pillars to mark each day of the brothers' entrance into the kingdom.

Outside, the dragons would feast on freshly killed deer and they would take to the sky and have their own games of jousting and charioteering, much to the amusement of the crowd below. That was before the hunters came and slowly destroyed the once-thriving community. Many died in an attempt to overthrow the hunters, the dragons falling victim to their weapons of sulphur and tar, their nets of steel, and huge barbed hooks that displaced the scales all too easily. Those were the worst times, and Bard remembered being hidden in the basement until it got too small for Sagitta and then the dragon would have to go and hide in the caves. His senses would come alive when his brother disappeared into the undercroft, and he could see that the natural cave opened up into pitch black where the scent of the earth was heavy and the hollow sound of dripping water echoed around him. Beneath his feet, mud glistened red against the glow of his scales, and a dug-out had been filled with sand as a resting place for the duration where Sagitta would stay until the all-clear sound was heard. But Sagitta had told him he could smell the silver that ran the length of the underground warrens, and if they could reach it, it could save them all. Bard considered that this is where the dragons of old found the precious silver that gave them longevity, strength, healing qualities, as well as a host of other properties—making the scales incredibly valuable. But when they decided to block up the silver and rely on venom only, the dragons began losing their fight against the hunters; for the weapons of man were becoming much more advanced and sophisticated.

Bard shuddered, for the conundrum was too gruesome to contemplate.

He reached out to his mother, but he couldn't find her, he couldn't send a message or find a channel of communication like he used to be able to. Maybe he was tired, perhaps his head was so full of information that he couldn't link up with her now. He didn't want to imagine that she had died in the battle. No, she was too powerful for that. Far too important, so he closed his heavy eyelids, sent a message of love to Sagitta, and finally dropped off to sleep.

CHAPTER NINE

The walls around the temple were as incredible as the
monolith itself and led into a garden of sizeable
proportion with vast geometric structures around it.
At the tip of each diagonal was a fountain that soared
into the air and lit up a different colour when the sun
was at its zenith. The structure was in the shape of a
star and a smaller replica of the palace where the quarters and training grounds came off the central hub and
divided into five points.

The temple was a small shrine, where every
member of the city was expected to visit at least once a
day. Here, they could have a quiet time of reflection
with the dragon gods or sit and marvel at the architecture. They could leave their writings in scrolls or gifts
they had made because this spiritual place was a direct

link to something unimaginable, something far removed from anything anyone had seen before.

The walls were built of huge, unworked limestone boulders which were roughly fitted together and smaller chunks of limestone filled the spaces. Inside the temple was a cool interior, and the plaster on the inner walls had been smoothed to a papyrus like quality. Four ornate pillars had been carved with images of dragons and other winged beings and stood sentinel at the corners of a richly decorated marble tomb. On top of the tomb was a solid gold sculpture, adorned with rare and precious gems. When the sun was at its zenith, a beam of spectral light filtered through the entrance and lit up the dragon sculpture and everything around it. On the walls were a range of hieroglyphics, codes and other ancient symbols, which scholars and academics had spent decades trying to decipher. More dragons and monoliths were strategically placed, and the muffled beat of tom-toms echoed continually round the enclosure.

Many thought that the muffled beats were a way of the 'old ones' to communicate with the living, for here they lay preserved in stone, waiting for the stars to align so they could resurrect themselves again. But until such time, they could only communicate with transmitted thought and summon the chosen ones to do their bidding.

❧ ❧ ❧

Bard was outside the opening, and after removing his slippers, he entered the sacred monolith by putting his palms together and bowing low to the golden dragon. He then lit two candles, one for his mother and one for his brother, and asked for continued health and good fortune. He sat down and listened to the beat of the drums, surreal in their very presence but so powerful in their divinity. Now, he was able to connect with his ancestors, and the gods in the sky, and all the individuals who had passed through these very doors and sat in this very spot. He closed his eyes and breathed in deeply, savouring every particle of the divine activity. He then pushed himself up, bowed low once again and backed out of the temple without taking his eyes off the tomb.

He just about managed to avoid bumping into Haynes who was putting his slippers to one side.

'I'm sorry, Haynes, I must have been in a bit of a trance.'

'Easy to do, Bard, once the mind is engaged with

the past it takes a few minutes to come back to the present.'

Bard smiled knowing exactly what he meant. 'How is Pyxis?'

Haynes stopped in his tracks, suddenly aware that Bard already knew something. 'How did you know that something was wrong?'

'I think most of the dragons are upset at the moment.'

'Why do you say that?'

'Because of the way that Ijja is treating Bellatrix.'

Haynes hung his head in anguish. 'That's why I am here, actually.'

'To ask the gods for guidance?'

'Yes, Mensa is distraught and Pyxis doesn't know what to do. Although colossal in size their voices are a drop in the ocean. We are so thankful for Sagitta who gives Bella the comfort she needs.'

'I know, Sagitta tells me every day to do something about it; but as we all know, it's only the Guardians that can act.'

'It's so unfair, the Guardians rarely see what's going on, and that idiot gets away with the continual cruelty.'

'Always the way though isn't it, the corrupt and the ignorant always go undetected.'

Haynes nodded, a sort of insufferable nod. 'But

that's why I am here today, I am going to spend some time with the dragon god, and through the power of thought I will explain how intolerable the situation has become.'

'I am glad. If enough people act on what they see; whether it's telling the Guardians, or Ser Alderman, or the gods, then something will get done. It has to.'

'It can't go on for much longer, Bard. Bella is getting more listless every day and it's only Sagitta that can lift her spirits.'

'Well, I don't have to tell him to do that; he loves her, he truly loves her. I will try and speak with one of the Guardians when I can.'

'Thank you, Bard. I will see you later for practice.'

'You most certainly will. I am off to the library for an hour or so to seek out some information. I do hope the gods are receptive to your plight.'

'They will be. Perhaps they are the only ones who can do anything.'

They bid their goodbyes and Bard went in the direction of the library. Another building of cyclopean architecture and he pushed at the doors which opened up yet another new world. Here, candelabras came to life, black and white marble floors went on for miles, large mahogany tables with red leather chairs sat heavy with people and books. There were mezzanines, balconies, bridges, ladders, railings, shelves, cupboards, and then the books—lots of them. Huge ones, small ones, thin ones, thick ones, out of reach ones, and pocket-sized ones. This was a city on its own made entirely of leather and paper.

After asking the librarian where to find what he was looking for, he staggered to a table with an armful of books over which his eyes just peeked. He laid them out in order of importance then began to sift through the pages, one after the other, his eyes furiously scanning the scrolls, his brain absorbing reams of information.

He thought that he knew everything there was to know about dragons, after all, he had grown up with them.

'Their eyesight is much better than ours,' his mother had told him. 'They are the perfect hunters, and when they get a prey in sight and they're hungry, that prey doesn't stand a chance.'

'Can I feed him?' Bard had enquired.

'No, I have taught him everything he needs to know. He can find his own food.'

'You taught him everything?'

'Yes, everything. You can groom him though, dragons love being groomed and pampered.'

'Does he understand what I am saying?'

'Of course he does, he's your brother, you will always have that special bond.'

So it was with great interest he started to pour through the huge books, discovering something new on each page.

More than those of any other species, a dragon's life cycle and life span shape its capabilities and character. Notwithstanding war and famine, even the shortest-lived dragon can expect to see a score of centuries and become adept in arcane abilities. Their life starts in the egg, and their life cycle will pass through stages of wyrmling, young, adult, elder and ancient. By the time they reach adulthood, most dragons have developed a natural instinct for parenting, and like many other animals, they will mate for life. Though rare, but not unlikely, to rear young before the adult phase is a foolhardy measure, therefore most will become sexually active during adulthood. By the time the dragon reaches the elder stage the instinct to raise young has gone.

Dragons lay eggs in small clutches—the nest is usually in a cave or a lair—in a mound or pit where the parents bury them in sand to keep them warm. Here they will turn them and talk to them to establish a bond while in the embryonic state. When a dragonet is ready to hatch, it begins feeding on the inside of the egg's shell, absorbing the remaining nutrients and weakening the shell. It can then use a claw or a beak to break through the protective housing.

A dragon is the most advanced predator in the history of evolution. Their skills are developed in the embryonic state from a deep-rooted ancestral knowledge, and the memories of prior generations continue to develop so accurately, that a dragon can find its way back to an ancestral home that has been vacated for hundreds of years. Though some eggs are abandoned for various reasons, a dragonet will recognise the one who raised him as its own kind and will adapt to the one who raises it. If another dragon raises it, the outcome is good, if another species takes on the role, then those dragons will take longer to hone their abilities. It still has the advantage of its inherited instincts, but the lack of a teacher makes perfecting abilities an arduous task. These types of relationships do not last long, because inevitably the dragon will seek out a mentor of its own kind.

Dragons prefer existing structures to live in, such as castles and palaces or large, cavernous caves. As they develop in power, knowledge and strength they might swarm with others to enjoy a collective home. Regardless of numbers, in its advancing years, a dragon will seek out wealth and begin to hoard treasures wherever its dwelling might be.

An ancient dragon is the most powerful creature to walk the earth. Its strength, knowledge and ancestral abilities are *born from a deep-rooted connection with the earth's very structure. Many seek out the scales of a dragon for they believe they contain the nutrients for unsurmountable strength and power, for everlasting life, and magical arcane gifts. These people are wrong in their assumptions and only serve to push the dragons further into inaccessible wastelands, or worse, extinction.*

A polite cough paused the scanning and the absorbing, and Bard looked up to see Saul standing in front of him looking exceptionally rested and in good health.

'I just wanted to say thank you for saving me,' said Saul.

Bard closed the book and leaned back in his chair. 'I'm glad I was able to help.'

'So am I, the connection you have with your dragon is amazing. I have never seen anything like that before.'

'It's my mother's influence, she made it all possible.'

'Well, I should be thanking your mother as well then.'

Saul looked over to what Bard was reading. 'Interesting stuff.' He nodded his head and jutted out his chin.

'Yes, it is. I was talking to Dram earlier and it piqued my curiosity.'

'Dragons and their Origins.'

Bard nodded. 'I didn't realise there were so many species, and that they lived for so long, or how they reproduced.'

'Smart beasts to be sure. We could learn a thing or two from them I know that.'

Bard nodded his head in agreement. 'Yes, that is true.'

'We live in dangerous times now. Too many seek to take from them what is not theirs. They see these dragons as an easy way to make money and sell the stolen by-products as luxuries that will be no good to anyone. When will they ever learn?'

Bard shook his head, which mirrored Saul's reaction. 'Probably never, looking back at how long ago these books were written and the dragons were facing the same type of threats. But we are fighting back now —and hopefully, it's not too late.'

'As long as the dragons are still around us, it is never too late.' Saul looked over to the sundial on the wall. 'It's time for afternoon practice, are you coming?'

'Yes, I am. Let me put these books away first, and I will join you.'

CHAPTER TEN

'The aerial stadium is probably the largest on the complex, and only the most proficient of riders can come here,' Saul began.

'I thought the pavilion was big where I saw the Dance of the Dragons and then the arena when you fell.' Bard felt bad reminding him.

Saul recognised the awkwardness and put an arm around him. 'It's all okay, and I survived to tell the tale, but let me tell you a bit about the stadium and this lesson.'

'Please do, I am keen to learn.'

'This particular discipline is based on some of the ancient writings that you may have seen in the library.'

Bard nodded his head.

'In some of these writings, we have learned how

the gods would ride around the night sky in chariots drawn by mythical beasts.'

'Yes, I have heard about them.'

'Well, we re-enact those findings and create them ourselves.'

'It sounds amazing, Saul.'

'It is. It's spectacular and adrenaline pumping to watch, but it's also very dangerous.'

'Why do the Officials put you through it then?'

'Many reasons. To engage with our primeval knowledge of fight or flight responses, to release those dormant energies that have been allowed to stagnate and fester. Plus, Bard, the Officials want us to connect with the gods and show them that we have an understanding of their rituals and beliefs and that we too wish to emulate that strength.'

'Which riders do that?'

'The best riders are selected so today we have Dom riding Lupus—*the wolf,* against Sli riding Antares,—*the stag.*'

'Can you tell me about the riders?'

'I know that Sli is from Sturt Manor, and he is an exceptional rider because he was the chief groom and ostler at the stables there. What he doesn't know about horses, isn't worth knowing. It's that connection with the beast, and power to control, that makes him an ideal candidate to be put against another tribune,' Saul explained.

'And he will be riding against Dom?'

'Yes.'

'Dom was a fisherman wasn't he?'

'Yes, he was.'

'Is that fair?'

'No, it's not fair, Bard, but it's strategy. The objective is to get Dom to learn from his opponent, so if there was an airborne attack, he would know what to do.'

'But that takes months, surely?'

'Exactly, but this isn't their first meeting. There have been several before this one, and Sli has won on every occasion. Come, let's watch.'

Around the arena were many Officials and Tribunes, keen to watch the exciting chariot race. They had seen this meeting many times before, and as these two competitors put on such a grand display, it was as much for entertainment as it was for practice and a platform of learning.

With no sign of the competitors, the crowd was brewing with excitement as a swirl of colour came from ten huge canisters positioned around the top levels. Clapping and shouting ensued, for they knew the session was imminent. The colours continued to blend in harmony when a sheet of mist descended from the heavens. The spectators looked up and saw more dyes released, which swirled and blended as simulated fire exploded through the spectrum. Then the drums started. A deep, slow, rhythmic pattern, which sent shivers down the spine and resonated with the beating hearts of every living creature. Another official joined in with the drumming, then another, until the lower floor was a cacophony of beating drums that built up to a crescendo. And only when the trickle of triangles eased out the heavy thrumming, did the competitors fly in.

Suddenly, the arena came to life, and coloured spotlights circled the dragons and their chariots. They flew a lap around the outer perimeter to announce their arrival, waving their hands and whipping the crowd to a frenzy, their dragons eventually rearing to a screeching halt, breathing out fire and holding their positions in mid-air. Antares pulled a red chariot, and his rider, Sli, wore a red helm and red cloak. Lupus pulled a golden chariot, and his rider, Dom, wore a golden helm and cloak. The two men saluted each other in the customary sign of unity, then signalled to the expectant crowd.

'This is a clean and fair race,' boomed the official.

'The first dragon to complete twenty laps will be declared the winner.'

'That sounds easy enough,' said Bard, relishing the excitement.

'You wait, they have various implements to set their opponent off course. It's a very skilful and calculated discipline.'

Saul stood with his arms folded, expectant of a good race. Bard started to chew at the nail on his thumb, worried about another fall.

The red chariot was first off the mark when the flag went down, and the first spear was thrown at the gold chariot after a few laps, but Dom managed to swerve out the way as the whispering blade missed his chariot by a breath. He watched it disappear to the depths below and regained his momentum. He positioned his first arrow and sent it straight back; it got stuck in the red chariot's wheel and unbalanced it, but Sli steadied himself and managed to clear it by hanging precariously over the edge. The crowd went wild at this death-defying stunt. He dragged himself back and proceeded to load something at the rear of the carrier. The sand, dust and dirt blown out from the rear obscured the challenger's vision. Dragons' eyes could withstand such debris, but humans' couldn't, so Dom had to pull down the visor on his helm which was hot and claustrophobic and impaired his view. The golden chariot surged through the meteoric bombardment as the red chariot sped away. Sli threw another spear—and missed again. Dom manoeuvred the gold chariot round the course as best as he could, and drew level as Sli sent a second arrow that lodged in the other wheel—this one stayed put.

The dragons were hurtling round now at top speed, and both carriages were thrown about as the shower of debris remained in the air for several laps. Dom aimed his catapult high—it seemed the only way to hit his target from the speeding vehicle—and his strong arm pulled the sling back as far as it would go. When it was released, a heavy rock was sent soaring through the air and found its target with a thud. The crowd gasped as it knocked the red chariot off course, but Sli still had another trick up his sleeve, and managed to join a hose to a tank of cold water and sprayed it over his opponent's dragon. This incensed Lupus, and he roared in retaliation and sped away at top speed to get the chill off his skin. Dom secured a tank of foam which was directed to the other male dragon as they passed by. Now both dragons were speeding around the enclosure shooting through water, foam, particles of sweat, froth, dirt and sand, to the ecstatic applause of the onlookers. The two charioteers remained focused and determined as they continued the race.

Sli started to swing a ball above his head to gain momentum, then he turned for a moment, focused on his unsuspecting rival, and let go of the rope. As it made contact, it exploded into a shower of ribbons and Lupus began to slow because his vision was impaired. Dom wasn't sure what to do at first, but as his dragon couldn't see, there was only one thing he could do, so he crawled out of his chariot to remove the streamers from Lupus' vision. Once he was on his neck, he removed the ribbons and spoke to him. 'Come on, boy, we can do this, you are the wolf remember, you are invincible and cunning and clever; you can win this!'

All through the manoeuvre, Sli was spraying the hose of water to try and unbalance his opponent and unsettle the dragon. But Lupus, driven by the encouragement and faith in his rider, found that extra bit of energy and stormed past Antares and over the finish line to the rapturous applause of those below. He sent a tunnel of fire into the air to acknowledge his win and a canopy of golden stars fell into the golden chariot and over his rider. He reared in the air with Dom still firmly in place.

Sli came up beside him and held up a clenched fist

as a sign of unity and acknowledgement of a worthy win. 'Tremendous riding, Dom,' he shouted over the noise. 'I threw everything at you on that ride, absolutely everything. You are a worthy winner.'

'I have learned much from you, Sli, and I thank you. We both do.'

Dom patted his dragon in triumphant elation and shook hands with his opponent.

CHAPTER ELEVEN

Mensa, the female dragon, mother to Bellatrix and Pyxis was not happy. She would not respond to anyone, and she certainly wouldn't take part in any training. She snapped at everyone who went near her, and her agile tail was guaranteed to deliver painful blows to the unwary though she seemed to have decided that making life difficult for Ramou was not going to get things changed. In fact, she had to get him on her side to get things changed.

'I will only comply with you if you comply with me,' she had started. 'I have told you repeatedly that Ijja is hurting Bellatrix and you won't do anything about it.'

'I understand your frustration, Mensa, but there is nothing I can do.'

'But he is deliberately hurting her, everyone can see, why can't you say something?'

'It's not my place to, Mensa. It's up to the Guardians to put in formal complaints. Not the Tribunes.'

'And why is that?'

'A tribune might be trying to cause trouble by deliberately naming and shaming another. I have to follow protocol.'

'I don't know why Ijja is like it, Ramou. Bellatrix is not a difficult dragon.'

'I know that. Bellatrix is the most amiable, gentle and passive dragon I have ever known. No one knows why Ijja torments her so.'

'I think he's frightened of her, he's scared of her power and size, so he thinks that by being rough with her and unkind to her that she will be submissive.'

Ramou nodded his head. 'I can see your logic.'

'He keeps her on that dreadful chain, and makes it tighter and tighter every day. She can't go out and feed because of it. She can't even move.'

'Well, if he is scared of her, then his plan is certainly working.'

'But it's not good, Ramou, the only time she can move is when she's in the air. Thankfully, I have seen the other dragons bringing food back for her. Without them, she would starve. But she needs to hunt for herself, to eat larger prey.'

'I will talk to a Guardian and see if we can get the chain removed.'

'Please do, Ramou. I hate to see her so morose with her head down all the time, it seems that only Sagitta can bring a sparkle to her unhappy life.'

'It's strange though because I have never seen Ijja act as if he was scared of her, in fact, it seems the complete opposite.'

'The boy is a fool, Ramou, a fool who will never admit to fear but I can see right through him. I have been around long enough to know a snivelling little coward when I see one, and I look at his pathetic stupid face every day when he comes in, but he doesn't fool me.'

'I agree with you, we all agree with you, Mensa. There is not one tribune who looks up to Ijja or agrees with anything that he does. I will speak to the Guardians. I promise.'

'And don't forget to tell the Guardians that because Ijja chains her up for such long periods that she is cold all the time. She can't move, she can't wallow, she can't do anything.'

Ramou already knew that Bellatrix went hungry and that she hadn't been properly cleaned or pampered in months. So cold, hungry and dirty, it was a wonder she hadn't tried to take off Ijja's head, fulfilling the fears that made him ill-treat her. Or quite possibly Ijja stupidly thought that by keeping Bellatrix hungry, he would be teaching her a lesson and would keep her in submission. But everyone knew that Ijja was totally incompetent and shouldn't be looking after a dragon.

'If I do that for you, will you return to practice sessions with me?'

'If you get that chain removed I will do anything you want me to.'

'Good, we have a deal.'

CHAPTER TWELVE

Bard woke earlier than usual, long before dawn, and lay in his bed thinking about the day ahead. It was his sixteenth birthday. His mother had shown him how to recognise his day of birth and on a clear day like today, it was easy to spot the formations. As the hour approached sunrise, he rose and dressed quickly and stood on the balcony to welcome the new day. The morning sun had just climbed over the mountains, and its bright rays, slanting down the western slopes, were washing the plains with golden light. He saw a few of the dragons fly overhead on their way to catch their first meal of the day. Ahead, were miles upon miles of pastureland and the dragons cast elongated shadows on the dew-damp grass. He saw Sagitta and felt his joy at the warmth of the summer sun on his back, his own shadow reaching all the way down to the glittering bends of a river below.

To Bard's left, the avenue of old, storm-blasted pine trees led to the forest, and beyond the forest was the spectacular dragon pool. He knew these trees well and often came to this place to be alone and look out over the boundless ocean to the very farthest edges of the horizon. Hundreds of steps had been cleaved into a hillside that led down to the shore, and a fixed rope was the only thing to stop a perilous fall down the vertical cliff. Below, the waves broke against the dark rocks when the tide came in and sent a rush of froth and foam into the air. This was the most southerly face of the complex. From here, there was nothing but sea and sky and a vast horizon. To the north was Storma Bay where the Mountain Dragons resided, and even further than that was the endless and impregnable Boreas Crown Mountain Range, known to many as the *'end of the world'* and home to the giant Ice Dragons.

The gold light of day was already turning red. All across the eastern sky, the stars were fading into the brightness, and the feathery bands of clouds were rimmed with scarlet. Then, there it was, a blazing crimson ball, bursting the band of sea and sky, hurling beams of brilliance across the water. He looked away and saw the red light on the trunks of the pine trees and the pillars of the dragon pool. A golden beam shone through the pillars and lit up the seated female at the end of the aisle. The day was transforming before him; with light, with power and with the knowledge of an ancient civilisation.

His stomach growled to remind him that breakfast would soon be served in the refectory, while his head reminded him to give thanks in the temple first. He slipped into his outdoor slippers and found his way to the base of the apartment blocks. He heard a sound behind him, and turning, startled, saw a figure hiding in the shadows.

'Who are you? What are you doing here?' The voice was hoarse and whispery.

Bard flushed and gave a respectful bow of his head to avert his eyes because coming out of the shadows was the Grandmaster. He had already been informed about the thick black veil that covered the face, the heavy purple cloak that covered the body, and the long black gloves that covered the hands, and that he wasn't allowed to stare or try and make eye contact.

'My name is Bard. I am going to the temple.'

'I do not usually see anyone at this hour.'

'I'm sorry, Grandmaster. It is my birthday and I wanted to give thanks for my good fortune.'

'How do you know it is your birthday?'

'My mother taught me how to work out the alignment of the sun with the stars.'

'Hmmm,' came the growl. 'This type of encounter contravenes all our rules but I'll let it go this time.'

'Thank you, Grandmaster.' Bard kept his eyes fixed on the ground.

'I am going to my private chapel now. There is someone there I need to speak to. You will not follow me. You will not tell anyone you saw me. This is our secret. Do you understand?'

'Of course, Grandmaster.'

'Good, I will see you later in the grand arena.' The Grandmaster nodded and silently slipped away.

❧ ❧ ❧

After two months at the Dragon Palace, Bard had learned there wasn't a single boy or man that hadn't been a tribune, fought in the air on a dragon or had one to one combat in all the disciplines. But the rules of that honour and privilege meant lots of practice with many weapons and devices, and on occasions, it was demanded that they demonstrated hand to hand combat in the grand arena to which the Grandmaster was invited alongside some of the Officials.

The Tribunes were ushered into the huge arena of yellow sand, and already seated in the theatre provided were the spectators—the colours of their cords ranking them—the Fellows, the Guardians, the Heralds, the Readers, the Temple Boys, the Sword Master, the Stewards, and Ser Alderman himself at the very front. Around them hung the gold embroideries of the old masters and the white-garbed ceremonial garments of the deceased Officials. The slow beat of drums and the climbing calls of trumpets were matched by the rumbling of the crowd.

The sparring hall was a vast circle, hundreds of metres in diameter, half covered with a dome and half open to the sky. The air took on the scents of lavender and patchouli, which, ironically, bearing in mind the purpose of the arena, served to give the place a feeling of peace and tranquillity. At the rear of the chamber stood a set of enormous golden doors that led to the infirmary.

'Candidates,' the Steward bawled from the gallery. 'Get into position.'

Everyone took their positions into one long line facing the front, and then from above, the trumpets sounded the arrival of the Grandmaster into the arena. Two servants carried a sedan into the enclosure, and a gloved hand trembled next to a curtain, allowing a partial view of the outside world. As usual, the long purple gown concealed the head and body and a thick hooded veil made any facial recognition impossible.

'You remember the order of events?' the Reader asked hurriedly to anyone who was listening. 'As you approach the throne, you must keep your head low. Do not look at the Grandmaster. You must heed this instruction as this is a sacred ritual. Do not lift your head at all while you are moving towards the throne, keep your eyes firmly on the ground. When you reach the white marker, you will stop, you will then drop to your knee and put your right hand on your heart. You count a slow ten, arise, and keeping your head low, return to your starting position. Is that clear?'

Everyone nodded.

'Then, you wait until you are summoned by the Imperial Herald.'

The Reader did a quick headcount, ticked off all the names on his list and then he was gone, and one more white robe was added to the spectator seats.

Each tribune made the long walk to the white marker, went down on one knee as instructed, then returned to their position to form the single long line at the back of the arena again. No doubt the time passed normally, but it felt as though each minute was long and drawn out and the wait was becoming more and more tense.

Soon, the Tribunes had all taken the knee, and the row now faced the Grandmaster from a distance. The veiled figure stood up and looked to the ceiling above decorated with all the different constellations in the night sky. The long purple tunic looked oversized on the shrunken frame, and a nod was delivered to the Sword Master who stood by a cabinet of deadly looking weapons. He bowed low to his superior, eyes flickering against the urge to open them and then straightened his back again as if a wooden rudis lay flat against his spine. The Grandmaster sat back on the throne and gestured to the next official.

The Imperial Herald ran out into the centre holding his gong high, the deep sonorous tone sounding like a death bell. 'Ijja and Ramou, take your places.'

The Sword Master stepped forward with the previously selected weapons. He bowed to the candidates, then to the Imperial Herald and finally to the Grandmaster before returning to his sentry position by the weapons cabinet.

In the centre, Ijja and Ramou bowed to each other over their sword hilts. The crowd subsided into expectant silence. Ijja swung his swords into starting posi-

tion, legs bent, hips square, then with a twist of both
wrists threw his swords into two whirring figures of
eight before freezing with one sword across his body
and the other just above his eyeline. Ramou didn't
have the inclination for such displays of exhibition-
ism; instead, he stepped forward with a swing to
disengage Ijja's position, but Ijja blocked the move
with the hilts of his swords. Ramou retreated and
stretched his limbs, Ijja pressed forward, the whirring
blades forcing Ramou into a defensive stance again.
Ijja's left-handed cut came down on the block and as
he spun around his right blade nicked his opponent's
shirt. Ramou looked to the Officials to intervene and
shook his head in protest when they didn't. Ijja
pressed forwards again, the rotating blades moving
towards Ramou's head. Ramou needed to block with
his right sword and swing his left into the less
protected gut area. He managed the block, but his
lower cut was too wild, the weight of his sword dragging him onto the wrong foot. He got back into his
game with a desperate twirl and precision cut that
landed the flat of his sword against Ijja's cheekbone.
The noise was like the crack on a wet rock. Ijja knew
that if he had wanted to, Ramou could have taken his
head off right there and then. He had to admit defeat.
He dropped his swords and put his arms across his

chest in a cross. That was one lesson learned and Ramou returned the gesture with a bow. As they returned to the line there was no animosity—for now anyway. The Reader was busy taking notes, looked at them both over gold-rimmed spectacles, and then signalled to the official.

The Imperial Herald returned to the centre. 'Candidate Bard, approach your opponent.'

There were shouts of encouragement from the other candidates. Bard sent a silent prayer to his mother and then to Sagitta to give him the strength that he needed. He was glad that he had taken an early breakfast and there was no food in his stomach to rise and choke him. He took one tentative step, still praying for strength, skill and endurance. The Sword Master moved in beside him and gave him his weapons, but Bard did not look at him—his focus would be broken, and then he would not stand a chance. The arena was quiet now, no stamping, no calls; only the desperate sound of his parched tongue trying to flick some saliva into a dry mouth. For a moment, the arena disappeared in a white panic. Bard stumbled, his focus snapped back by the sudden flare of the moonstones and jade on his hilts. Each gem exuded a bright light from within and Bard was suddenly transfixed. Something began to change. Power rising from steel and silver. A lifetime of fighting. A dynasty of knowledge. He saw Sagitta in his mind's eye, transmitting knowledge that he needed to be aware of. It worked, and his mind stayed focused. He looked down at his tightly curled hand. He had never been taught to hold a sword like that. Fellow135 stepped into the combat area and bowed before him. Bard matched his movement and felt his stomach churning once again.

'Stance position,' Fellow135 said, taking his position with the sun behind him. He twirled his swords out and around his body in a mesmerising display, then held them there across his body.

Bard mirrored his stance. 'Fellow135,' he whispered behind the crossbar of the swords. 'Why am I fighting you? Why can't I fight one of my peers?'

'This is not a choice, Bard. The Grandmaster has requested it.'

Bard gulped hard remembering their brief encounter earlier that morning. 'Why?'

Fellow135 looked at him sternly. 'I do not know the reason, and I do not ask. I have to do as I am told, as do you.'

'I'm sorry.'

'I would see that as an honour, Bard, that the

Grandmaster has requested this match. The Grand-master must have seen something in you.'

Bard nodded his head and felt the eyes of the arena burning into his soul.

'Are you ready now?'

Bard took in a deep breath. 'Yes, I am ready.'

'Then show the Grandmaster what is expected of you and do not disappoint.'

Fellow135 raised his two swords. Angled for slic-ing, they came whirring at Bard's chest, but his block was simple, a step back of the back leg, a shift of weight, his right sword joining the left in front of him, crossing at the hilt, and holding firm in defence. The Fellow's blades cut deep but Bard held his grip firm as the face of determination glared back. Bard pushed down to release the force and the left sword lifted as the right made a swing for his opponent's throat. He was fired up now and the spectators started to chant for him. The Fellow smiled wryly. Bard started to twirl his swords as the Fellow retreated and refocused. Bard's eyes burned with power.

'I thought you said you didn't want to fight me,' the Fellow hissed.

'I didn't, but now I am focused, I am more prepared.'

'Good, sometimes that's all that's needed.'

The Fellow came at him, his swords raised high above his head. Bard braced, raising his swords just in time. The crashing force of steel against steel rang out across the arena. The Fellow's hilts locked down with his own, it was a stalemate, neither opponent wanting to yield, but then a voice came to Bard, telling him what to do. It was faint but powerful at the same time, like an ancestor instructing him. He sprang into action and released the locked hilts. His swords were a blur, a flash of metal controlled by another force. The Fellow pressed forwards. Bard now needed to execute a two-strike challenge. He managed the first part, but the second manoeuvre was clumsy and the Fellow was able to gain the advantage. His two swords locked into Bard's once more. Bard dug the side of his foot into the sand to stop the slide, and then something changed again. Bard knew what to do. Through a deep ancestral knowledge, his muscles and responses merged. He stepped backwards, pulling the swords with him, turning them in a backhanded sweep and raised them high above his head in an arch to get maximum impact. He could easily have taken the Fellow's head clean from his shoulders in one strike, but he didn't, instead, he stopped—suddenly. He bowed low without taking his eyes off his opponent. The crowd was ecstatic when the Fellow bowed with him.

'You fight well, Bard.'

'Thank you, Fellow135, I have trained hard.'

'I can see that, and I am pleased.'

The Fellow moved even closer in a respectful embrace and whispered. 'You know that, eventually, they will come. In large enough numbers they will get what they came for. You do know that.'

'I know they will come,' Bard responded quietly. He looked up to meet the Fellow's eyes and a boyish grin spread over his face. 'But they think all they'll face is a bunch of kids and some raging dragons. But when they see how far we've come, what they'll get may not be at all what they were expecting.'

Fellow135 bowed deeper. 'I hope you are right, Bard. I really hope you are right.'

CHAPTER THIRTEEN

Lepus flew again. Not gracefully, not easily, but she flew. With every flap of her wings, pain echoed each beat. Finding food had been hard and exhausted her quickly. Because of her young age, she had healed quickly, but she still had a lot of learning to do. She had seen a group of alligators in a river and caught one, a small one but the fight with it had been arduous and she had to take to the air quickly to escape the wrath of the mother. If she had been stronger it wouldn't have been such an ordeal, but with an injured wing that was only half working, she couldn't take any chances. But she had to. Driven by desperation, knowing there was someone else who needed her, she had to take whatever chances she could.

❧ ❧ ❧

It was warm here, thankfully. The paths were over-grown with sprawling flora, though a frost would sparkle in the moonlight and the tall stems would sway like stiff white whiskers. Drifts of dust had piled up against the castle walls, filling every nook and cranny. When the frost had disappeared the trees opened up their branches like a huge welcoming candelabra. Posies lay about the wide trunks in scintil-lating colours of the rainbow. The corvids had come together here, for a feast awaited them in numbers. The reminders of a bitter battle and heavy losses were prevalent, for between the trees lay grey ash and cinders, and here and there a blackened pile of bones with blistered skin and follicles of hair still attached. Though, after several months of feasting, it was grad-ually disappearing, with white maggots munching their way through the rotting corpses. However, the river ran pure and Zmeitsa had managed to crawl to its perimeter and had lowered her punctured frame into it. The infection was spreading, taking a toll on her body. She felt so weak, and the pain stabbed through her when she moved, so she gave up the effort and stayed in the water. All around the wounded areas, her scales were beginning to slip, leaving the exposed skin soft and painful. She dreamed of desecrated palaces and the smells of blood and burnt flesh. The air was full of tar, sulphur and toxic acid. For a long time, there was groaning and whimpering around her, and occasionally a human cry of pain would wake her from her slumber. The smoke in the air made her eyes water, so she tried to keep them shut, but when she slept for a long time, she awoke with her eyes glued together and had to snort mucus from her nostrils. She was hungry constantly, but no matter how much she ate, she took no strength from her food. Everything was a task; everything was painful and difficult. She had almost lost the will to live. Almost, because she loved waking up to see her home still standing—Castle Dru in Durundal, its slender spires and towers disappearing into the clouds, the graceful buttresses, delicate arches, fluted columns, terraces and bowers. The windows sparkled in the daylight and the high stone walls girthed the perimeter. She groaned a heavy sigh and remembered that there was laughter once, the gardens were bright with flowers and the fountain gushed silver droplets every day. She thought of Bard, playing in those very gardens with Sagitta, and felt a rage burning inside towards those consumed with avarice as a tear ran down her face. Her sons, strong sons, with good hearts. The thought of them brought back a memory.

⁂

The morning air was dark with the smell of rain, and the dragons peered out from their stone surroundings as if they were looking directly at him. A cloud seemed to hang over him today, ragged and black as his cloak. A young man paced about restlessly, muttering to himself, and the coven of witches trembled when he brushed past them. He was agitated about something, he did not know what, he just knew that he needed a change.

Outside, he heard the waves crashing against the jagged rocks, eager to get past the mouth of the cave. The wind picked up pace and threaded its way through the canyon into the dome of dragons where it curled around the hundred faces and breathed energy into them. 'Zmeitsa, Zmeitsa.' The wind whispered a name. He caught his breath and spun around. He heard the name again. 'Zmeitsa, Zmeitsa.'

Then a fierce light exploded in front of him.

He shielded his eyes and felt his breath caught in his throat. One hand gripped his neck and the other protected him from the glare. As the surge of power settled down, it went pitch black.

'What witchcraft is this?' his voice quivered.

All he could hear was the sound of his breathing; loud, anxious, agitated. He tried to calm himself. A tremendous roar was followed by a funnel of fire, and out of the flames stepped a creature so hideous he thought he would die right there and then. He backed away, stumbling, slipping, falling on the stones but the firelight paralysed him and he couldn't move. The scaly image grew taller as the ashes around its feet lifted in a frenzy and swirled around the body before disappearing into the orifice of a throat. The green skin became flesh-toned. Long golden hair grew from the crown of its head, and what could only be described as a dragon's body, became human form: young, lithe and beautiful. A naked woman stood before him, veiled in plumes of smoke and exhaling the last remnants of fire. She blinked slowly as she regarded him, reptilian amber eyes burning bright with flames as she spoke.

'Segan Hezekiah, I have watched you grow into a man, I have seen the change in you; from the young, timid boy into a man of culture and knowledge. I can see that you have a fire burning within your soul, an energy that will take you on a great adventure and beyond your wildest expectations.'

Segan pinched himself and shook his head, not quite believing what was in front of him or what he had just heard.

'I can see that you are strong and courageous, and I can help you become even stronger.'

'How?' his voice was small and weak like a child's.

'The gods of darkness protect you.'

Segan laughed out loud.

The fire roared, the wind howled, the amber eyes glared. 'Do not mock me!' she bellowed.

He swallowed the laugh and spoke quietly. 'Why would you do that for me?'

'Because I want something in return.'

He braced himself, fearful of what she would request from him.

'What can I give you?' He heard the whisper.

Her eyes burned brighter, the plumes of smoke clung to her curves. The breeze curled around his torso whispering her name. 'Zmeitsa, Zmeitsa.'

She bore into his very soul. He turned away.

'Look at me, Segan Hezekiah.'

Their eyes met.

'It is written that two life forms will charge through the kingdoms and seek vengeance for those who have been slain and tortured. These males will be born from the seed of a mortal and the womb of a dragon.'

Segan furrowed his brow in astonishment.

'Their purpose is to bring peace.'

His rhetoric was mocking. 'That is impossible.'The fire blinded him. The wind froze him to the spot.

He frowned.

'I want you to father these males, for one will be in the form of a dragon, and the other in the form of a human.'

She saw the pink cavern of his mouth.

'If you do this for me then I give you my word, no man will take your life.'

'How do I know you are speaking the truth?'

The fire roared again, the waves snarled foam around the cavern, the wind raced through the gloom, but Segan had found his strong voice.

'Will I ever be able to see my sons?'

'No, never, and it is not your concern. The boys will be mine and given everything they need—I can assure you of that.' Her voice became more impatient. 'No more questions. I grow weak in this life form... I am tiring as we speak... now do we have a bargain?'

ชื่ ชื่ ชื่

She sat looking at the view with happy memories tumbling in her head when she heard the sound of heavy wings approaching. She knew who it was and smiled.

Lepus flew down with the life-giving nectar. 'I have what you need, Zmeitsa.'

'Thank you, Lepus, though I fear my recovery will be long and your journeys will be many.'

'I don't mind, you know I don't mind, but that's why we need to stay in dragon form, our human form takes up too much energy.'

'I know, though I fear I will never return to human form again.'

'Nonsense, I have been collecting the stones and can see they are doing their job.'

'Thank you, child. I can feel myself getting better.'

As the old dressings were removed and the new unguent applied, Zmeitsa lapsed into a semi-dream-like state and she saw a vision.

≈ ≈ ≈

Deep in the heart of the mountain, men walked alone carrying lanterns and pickaxes. The glow stretched ahead into the dark tunnels and created huge, disfigured shadows on the walls. Year after year, Break Pass Ridge slaves cleaved deeper into the living rock, tunnelling into the heart of the mountain, discovering fresh arteries and closed veins, where they would pick out precious stones and barrels full of gold. Segan Hezekiah made them excavate more and more until the mountain range became cancerous with sores. Many thought it would crumble one day. But if that ever happened, it would take Segan Hezekiah with it, and end the torture for good.

The slaves were always covered in white rock dust. They were hunched and weak, with skin like thin grey paper as they never saw the light of day. But the more they excavated, the warmer it became, and Hezekiah was confident the fire of life simmered somewhere below—and once the tunnellers exposed it, he would move his throne room closer, and breathe in the life-giving embers daily. For now, though, his throne room was comfortable and warm from a man-sized hearth and rimmed with a thousand illuminated candles that danced and flickered in this reluctant womb.

Cornelius was led into the chamber of the mountain king. This spacious room held little in the way of furniture —its grandeur was manifested in its construction rather than its content. White marble columns rose from the mosaic floor to a gilded ceiling, and the finest gold leaf prints lined the walls. Niches and arched windows were patterned with intricate carvings, and silk rugs covered the floor. Dim lamps carved into the rock, and illuminated decanters full of vintage wines. The servant didn't even look up as he shuffled over to a marble stand. He took a gem-encrusted goblet and poured a claret for his master.

Hezekiah sat at a dark wooden table with a platter of

food in front of him. He chewed menacingly on a haunch of deer as the goblet of wine was placed at his elbow.

From a crack between the flagstones, a spider, disturbed by the shuffling, scuttled towards the edge of the room and settled at the base of a large wooden plinth. Atop the perch above, a hawk, tethered and hooded, cocked its head, aware of the eight-legged intruder. It flapped its wings and screeched loudly. Hezekiah reached for a catapult, nocked a plum-stone in the sling, and hit the spider straight on, then threw a piece of meat into the mouth of the hooded hunter. He then turned thirty degrees, and fixed his eyes on a large, ancient, leather-bound book, left open on a gold inlay desk. The pages were of the highest quality waxed vellum, and contained writing, verses, figures and motifs. It was of little interest to the spider—but the bird had done its job. Hezekiah cocked his head, smiled, and went back to his meal.

The prisoner couldn't remember when he had last eaten. His body was all wiry muscle and sinew, and his ribs clung on to even thinner skin. His matted hair and beard disguised the once handsome face. He could feel his mouth salivate and his empty stomach rumble as the sweet aroma of meat fat and dripping wafted into his sensory glands.

Hezekiah, who preferred to be referred to as the Mountain King, looked up and pushed his plate away. He wiped his mouth with the back of his hand and sat back in his throne. He nodded to the guards who stepped forward and presented Cornelius to him.

'I hear that the prisoner escaped.' He picked something out of his teeth, looked at it and put it back into his mouth.

'I am sorry, my lord, we searched for miles but he was nowhere to be found. He must have died in the freeze.'

'No matter,' said the king. 'I see we have a younger, fitter, more able replacement anyway.'

'Yes my lord, we thought you would be pleased.'

The king stood up and walked towards Cornelius. His voluminous black velvet robe was trimmed at the collar with the pelt of a grey wolf and settled into nice, neat folds when he stopped moving. He was of average height and average build, with a square face and deep-set eyes. His tamed beard and curly hair concealed most of his features, and a small crown was wedged on his forehead. He didn't look old, he didn't look that young either. The most striking character-istic about him was the deep blue eyes that could melt the ice off the top of the mountain it seemed. And despite the tales that Cornelius had heard, he didn't look like a terrifying ogre at all; but then again, more often than not, they were the worst types he feared.

⁂

'Cornelius and Segan. They will meet each other, they will know each other.'

'Calm yourself, Zmeitsa, calm yourself, you are using up too much energy.'

'But I didn't know, I didn't know that they would meet each other.'

'You are delirious, Zmeitsa. Here, I have made some of your favourite lavender oil to smooth on your skin, let me tend to your aches and pains.'

The oils worked their magic as Lepus smoothed the lotion onto the wounds and Zmeitsa relaxed again.

'That's better, you need to stay calm so that you can get better.'

'Yes, you are right, Lepus. Thank the gods that you are here to take care of me.'

'Always, Zmeitsa, always.'

❧ ❧ ❧

Her mind raced again. She saw pictures, words, everything merged together. She saw a woman, thinking of her brother. The woman was upset, she had seen her brother slain: *She'd seen him dying at the hands of the blade. The woman screamed. The power surged through her veins, and she roared like a warrior summoning all the strength she had.*

Segan turned round—shocked, aghast. He hadn't expected this from a woman. His mouth was wide open in bewilderment. She broke free of her constraints and in a blur of speed, she withdrew her knife and plunged it into Hezekiah's heart. Then she swung around and sliced the jugulars of the guards behind her.

≈ ≈ ≈

'The girl will kill him. My prophecy is right, *no man will take your life.* I never said a woman couldn't.'

Lepus nuzzled her. 'Poor, Zmeitsa, so much tar and sulphur in your body has made you hallucinate. Better that than death though. I will stay with you again tonight and collect more stones in the morning.'

≈ ≈ ≈

Zmeitsa's eyes flew open. 'Lepus, you know something. You have seen something that you don't want me to know about! But you must tell me… and tell me now!!'

CHAPTER FOURTEEN

2 months previously ...

After two days, Lepus began to see things: dragons with spiderweb wings, demons with clawed feet, and corvids with blades for claws and perilous hooks for beaks. She saw feasts of forbidden delicacies and could smell meat that stank of a week-old carcass. When she saw them she thought of her mother. But closing her eyes did not remove her sight, she still saw these images. After a while, she could not tell if her eyes were open or shut. Throughout the day it occurred to her that she might be dead. Nothing made any sense anymore and her dreams were becoming more confusing. The strange noises were always apparent and she longed to wake up somewhere she wasn't delirious.

᠎᠎᠎

When she was little she would often see the dragons in flight, their shadows falling over her as they passed above. Some of her friends were frightened by the shadows and went to hide in the barns—those friends would remain in human form. But her mother had always told her that she was special, and soon she would have the power to choose what she wanted to be. From that moment on, Lepus couldn't wait for the day when she could finally shift to become a dragon. In dragon form, she would be stronger, more resilient, and more intuitive. She could fly, she could roar, she could send out flames of burning fire. But even dragons were mortal, and many had perished at the hands of the hunters, including her own family. Sorrow brought her to her senses again, and realising that hunger was her most insistent need, she shook the hallucinations from her thoughts and began to search for survivors and food.

At first, she couldn't see anything and thought she was the only one who had survived the attack. She had listened to the sounds of the men dying but feared moving in case it was a ruse to ambush the dragons again. When the crying and moaning stopped that's when she looked around and discovered that everyone had perished apart from Zmeitsa. She'd tried to help her sisters, but they had died instantly from their horrific wounds; though judging by the wailing, the hunters had taken a lot longer.

By the time Lepus returned to the clearing by the river, the only sound in the forest was the constant staccato of water dripping from leaves. Her golden eyes glowed in the trickles of sunlight seeping through the breaking clouds.

It was three days after the battle and she was still nursing an injured wing. She had taken to the air and flew to her usual feeding ground. Food was always plentiful here and she needed more food than ever now. But on this particular day, she noticed a patch of mud that seemed different than it had before. There was a handprint and the skid of a boot that was no more than a few days old.

The hunter fell and had difficulty regaining his footing. She thought that possibly an alligator had taken the hunter by surprise, but following the prints to a thicket with several bent branches, she saw the same footprint embedded in the undergrowth. She scanned the area for more clues and noticed blood on the trunk of a tree and that the larger branches had mud on where he had climbed to an elevated position. Further inspection detected the fibre from a woollen shirt and the bloodied print of a hand on the higher branches. Maybe he had rested here after the attack or maybe he was waiting for more survivors to join him. She crouched down on all fours, her belly touching the ground. The young dragon moved in a slow, sinuous, crawl, sniffing the ground carefully, tilted her head, then crawled forward, paused and sniffed again. She continued this methodical examination, moving further into the forest when she picked up the scent of another hunter.

This one had come a different way after the attack, or maybe had even been waiting for the injured hunters to come back. She looked around for wagon tracks, the only means of transport for handling a bounty of dragon scales, and chased the tracks through the forest. The trees were thick here, but each branch, each twig, each leaf had the telltale signs of intruders. She continued her search and came to an ancient road that she had never seen before. Here, it was unnaturally quiet, but in the distance, she saw a blue-green river shining in the morning sun. Reeds grew thick in the shallows along the banks, and Lepus spotted a wild boar drinking. Silently she stalked it and by the time the boar had noticed the huge black shadow getting ominously closer, it was too late; the jaws caged it and swallowed it in one go. The water was warm here and she plunged her head in to wash off the blood, the hairs and the dirt, and that's when she spotted the dead man caught up on a rotting log. The body of a hunter, white, shapeless and swollen; his murderous bows still shouldered, blood congealed on his cloak and a school of fish nibbling away at the exposed skin.

She took to the air again and, following the old road, glimpsed a forester's cabin surrounded by trees. Here, there was evidence of men seated around a fire. The dragon scales and wagon had been abandoned. Makeshift bloodied bandages were smouldering on the embers. Her eyes darted around, her ears set to high alert, but all she detected was a gentle breeze rustling through the trees. What did they flee from? Where did they go? She hunted around for more clues, but could only see the footprints heading in a northerly direction. And then she got the whiff of something in the air, something that piqued her interest, and foregoing all fear she decided to land. The smell was arousing deep ancestral knowledge, and a connection to a higher power was ever-present. She followed the odour to a large circular structure protruding from the ground. Here, the smell was strongest and she peered into the mouth of the well-head to discover a tunnel of blackness. Her clawed hand was on a chain, and she knew she would have to use the chain to climb down the shaft to see what was at the bottom. She wrapped her talons around the links and using her hind legs to counterbalance, the darkness swallowed her as she made the descent. As the sphere at the top got smaller, the chill began to hinder her progress. *I need to act fast for my muscles will start to seize up in the cold.* But then she was aware of a liquid running down the shaft; a metallic, shiny substance that somehow she knew had life-saving qualities. It was coming through the masonry and collecting in clumps on the boulders. She didn't know how she knew, but she knew she needed this metal. A bucket was at the bottom of the shaft and she clawed at the clumps on the walls and put as much as she could into the vessel. Then climbing back up the well, holding on to the chain with one talon and the bucket with another, the whispers of a time gone by echoed round the enclosure.

❧ ❧ ❧

'*The Mother of Durundal needs the silver. Place the rocks on*

her body, then she will heal. Do not fear what you see, little
one, for the greatest challenge is in the first few minutes. Do
not abandon our Mother. We all need her.'

🐾 🐾 🐾

Back at River Dru, Lepus placed the rocks on
Zmeitsa's body, and repelled when she saw how it
melted the wounds and began to crystallise on her
iridescent golden scales. Lepus kept her distance as the
dead flesh slipped from the Mother's skin and pooled
into the soil as foul-smelling rotten slime but the
wounds started to heal and the puncture marks began
to close.

Lepus had to make several trips to the shaft to
bring Zmeitsa back from the dead. She tried putting
the stones on the other dragons but it didn't work. It
was only herself and the Mother who reacted to the
healing silver. Over the next few weeks, Zmeitsa got
stronger, her torn flesh became thin, silvery grey scars
and then they finally disappeared altogether. Her
breathing became less laboured, her eyes less glassy.
Then one day, her eyes flew open and she gulped in
great breaths of fresh air, like a fish out of water. Her
senses were alive, her blood raced through her body,
her instinct was aroused, and then she knew…

'Lepus, you know something. You have seen something that you don't want me to know about! But you must tell me... and tell me now!!'

Lepus explained what she had seen.

❧ ❧ ❧

'The hunters were inches away from something that could have brought them wealth?' Zmeitsa shook her head in pity at the prospect of the human race but applauded the dragons' good fortune. 'All our lives depend on silver in one way or another.'

'It would seem that way, but I noticed the smell of metal, they probably couldn't.'

'That's because we are so much more advanced.' Zmeitsa licked at the silver drops on her talons.

'But there was a voice telling me what to do. I felt this pull, like a magnet drawing me inside the shaft.'

Zmeitsa stopped licking her claws. 'Something like an electromagnetic pull?'

Lepus nodded her head as if it was she who had made the connection. 'Yes, yes it was, and the smell of metal was overpowering.'

Zmeitsa nodded her head in reverie. 'I do not have a memory of how or when the well was dug, but I do know that there are many of these shafts around the estate. They intersect with each other, offering miles upon miles of corridors and passageways all combining in a labyrinth that passes through the mountains. In fact, one of the tunnels can be accessed from a room in the castle, an escape route that leads to a cave at the base of The Giant's Claw mountain range.'

'So why haven't we used it to escape?'

'As dragons, we are too big, as a woman, I will not run away.'

'Who or what built them?'

'Who do you think?'

'A superior race?'

Zmeitsa breathed in deeply. 'Yes, and I know that these tunnels and shafts were put here for dragons. The silver gives us power, it extends our lives and helps us to create our venom. It keeps our scales strong, through threads on the outer membranes.'

'Is that why the hunters take our scales?'

'Most probably, Lepus. Somewhere in an ancient document, there is evidence of silver in dragon scales, and the hunting has become rife again. What we used in the last attack, we were born with. We inherited it from our mothers and our fathers, just like the fire that is within us. But now we need more silver. Lepus, my dearest, you were led to it, so I know we are being summoned.'

'How do you know that?'

'I can feel it. I felt it many times summoning Bard. But this time it's much stronger.'

Lepus looked at her, puzzled; but Zmeitsa was the Mother of Durundal, and as the Mother of Durundal she knew everything. Lepus didn't want to ask how she knew what it was, or why she'd ignored the call for Bard to fulfil his destiny—she probably wouldn't understand anyway. Instead, she simply asked: 'What shall we do?'

'We will excavate the rocks from the mine and we'll grind it down with our talons and our teeth.'

'Why do we need so much silver?'

'Because we are going to war, Lepus, and we need as much ammunition as we can carry; to make more venom and to heal the other dragons and ourselves.'

Lepus suddenly saw the urgency. 'I can do that while you are getting stronger.'

'Good girl, now tell me which direction the hunters were going?'

'North, definitely north.'

'You didn't see how many though?'

'No, I didn't want to get too close and have them

come back here to finish us off, but from the prints, I would say about six.'

'Six you say. They must be meeting up with more hunters further along the dragon trail, and that means they will be heading for the Mountain Dragons and then the Grand Palace in the constellation of Hercules.'

Lepus looked at the Mother's emaciated body. 'You are still not well enough to fly, Zmeitsa.'

'I know, but we have time. They are on foot, remember, and probably injured. And now I have to make sure I get better—fast. And when I am stronger, there is someone I need to see.'

CHAPTER FIFTEEN

On this particular day, a drill had been planned without the prior knowledge of the Tribunes. The siren bellowed as the sun began to set, and within seconds everyone started for their stations and the Officials stood on the highest tier of the lighthouse with their telescopes pointed to the sky. Then, above the wind, came the flapping of gigantic wings. Long shadows raced across the enclosure as dragons spiralled from the sky, spreading their wings to descend with downy grace in the centre. Sagitta was the first to land, his outstretched wings nearly blocking from sight his friend Bellatrix, who touched down quietly behind him. Sagitta was radiant. The crimson of his open wings blended with the sunset behind him as if all the sky were part of his being.

Light played on every scale and turned them iridescent. He stretched and relaxed the long, powerful talons on all four feet, displaying sharp claws that were golden. The crowd nodded with silent approval at the display. Bard stood proud as he greeted his brother. Bellatrix made no such display, keeping her wings folded and her sad eyes fixed on the floor. Ijja glared at her.

'Stupid dragon,' he snarled. 'What's wrong with her now?'

She felt his dismay and tried to make herself even smaller as he approached.

'Do I have to bow to you, oh weak and feeble one, do you think we are all in your shadow and should kneel before your incandescence?' He shook his head.

Bellatrix backed away when she saw the collar.

'Come here, you stupid creature, at least you respond to this.'

Bard saw the smoke coming from Sagitta's mouth as he watched the events unfolding; a troubled dragon would not perform well. He went up to Ijja and touched his arm.

'Praise her, Ijja, she is only young.'

Ijja muttered something under his breath and continued to be heavy-handed with the young female.

Bard could only shrug as he caught Sagitta's watchful eye. There was nothing he could do.

'You will obey me!' Ijja's command came out like a roar, full of spittle and fury.

Sagitta could not bear to watch and yet he could not tear his eyes from her. He could feel her terror as Ijja commanded her to fly. He knew how she struggled to pull her body into alignment when she wasn't focused. Then he heard her wings beating as she began to work her muscles and she was gone.

Dragons were now streaming in from every feeding ground outside the palace and every access within the enclosure, their riders struggling into fighting gear and securing appropriate weapons. The Guardians checked to see if there were enough riders assembled and mounted to make up a full squadron. Timing was of the essence here and the Head Guardian hesitated long enough to have the Temple Boys tell every tribune the importance of this mission and how it was to be approached like a real attack. A few of the dragons had already skimmed the forest to get quick bearings and seek out the targets before they soared up with their riders to begin the attack.

Incredibly, Ser Alderman believed they had actually managed to beat their own previous time of getting into the air. Then a dragon roared directly above the temple with its rider in position. As Ser Alderman glanced upward to identify the beast, he noticed Bellatrix and Ijja going in the direction where the awful cold would impede their speed. He tutted into his notebook. Valuable lessons would be learned that day and this matter would be fully addressed in the next meeting. They couldn't risk losing a dragon. Unless it was a ploy to lure the enemy—the riders had to be much more careful. He would have to investigate. But the anomaly bothered him.

🐾 🐾 🐾

In the distance, Ijja could see the mountains of Storma Bay rising steeply from the northern plain, setting their jagged peaks like teeth against the cold blue of the sky, while to the south, the lowlands rose and undulated gently across the horizon then slowly descended as rolling green hills into the wastelands. From his height on the back of the dragon, he could see the multitude of rivers flowing across the land like fine silver threads stitched into an emerald cloth. But the further they flew towards the mountains of Storma Bay, the colder it became.

Bellatrix hated flying in the cold. She disliked the way it impaired her vision and loathed the way her wings tightened in the lower temperatures. Yet she knew that Ijja had done this deliberately. With the choking collar around her neck, he knew that she needed heat, and this was a punishment for her sullen behaviour. She tried to send a message out to Sagitta, but the cold had rendered her communication powers useless. She felt the heat from Ijja's body and tried to direct it into her muscles. *He knows that I will be suffering. He knows that I will tire easily in these unbearable conditions. Why did I end up with such a callous rider?* She blinked to keep the cold from freezing her eyelids together and exuded a plume of smoke to keep her face warm; which it did for a little while, but with relentless certainty, the further she flew, the colder it became. Storma Bay was looming up before them, a mixture of forests and caverns amongst the jagged peaks. The Mountain Dragons lived there, in a city within the forest, with heated caves and indoor waterfalls, it was a haven for those who lived there. As they flew on, the mournful wail of a lone wolf echoed below them. Snow had recently fallen, and they were out of range to signal for help should they run into trouble. But Ijja couldn't care less and kept her collar tight to make her fly further towards the mountains. However, she was tiring, and even with the collar digging into her neck, she knew she had to rest—for this rider wouldn't stop until he had been out for half the night.

'What are you stopping for, you useless creature? I didn't say we could stop!' He pulled the collar tighter so she couldn't breathe. 'Get back in the air you pathetic beast.'

But her legs came down to land and she crunched into the soft snow in a small clearing and hung her head in exhaustion. Her eyes partially closed and she was able to breathe more easily in the lower altitude. The howling broke out again, descending through the octaves to a deep and sonorous moan. *She's warning me of something.* Bellatrix opened her eyes and saw a maze of footprints, a burnt-out firepit, and blood in the snow.

A slain dragon hung in the crook of a tree. It was a Mountain Dragon, and judging by the smell it had been hanging there for days. Stripped of its scales, it made for a sorry sight, with a single arrow jutting from its side. Bellatrix trembled, and her eyes flared wide, looking for further signs of murder. And there, not two metres away from where she stood, another arrow-riddled, scaleless body lay hacked and tortured to death. Bellatrix moved closer and nudged its lifeless body—she had never seen one of her own kind in such a state before. Never seen a dead dragon with its scales and tongue cut off. She knew that Ijja was petrified as he cursed her and hit her repeatedly, demanding she get back in the air—she ignored the brutal collar as it dug deeper into her throat without a pause. She cared about her fellow species and needed to show her respect, and as she took another swipe to the head, a single tear dropped onto the dead dragon's flayed body. When she was ready to leave, she took to the sky with Ijja's barrage of abuse ringing in her ears.

'Fly faster, you imbecile, I have to tell Ser Alderman what I have found.'

ঙ ঙ ঙ

Sagitta and Bard were among the first in the air, and the dragon craned his long neck around in a wide sweep, eyeing the forest as he had been instructed; then, with a warning to Bard, he folded his wings and dove towards an especially thick patch, braking his descent with neck-snapping speed. As Sagitta belched fire, Bard watched, grinning with intense satisfaction as a huge expanse was torched and the target crumbled to cinders in a matter of seconds. Another dragon was hot on his tail, ready to blast if there was a counterattack and another target sprang up as a replacement. Gouts of flame were blossoming across the sky, protecting each other, looking out for each other, working as a team. The sun glinted off green, blue, red and bronze backs as dragons veered, soared, dove and breathed fire onto targets that represented the hunters. On the ramparts, the selected Guardians kept a tally of the casualties, others traced the formation, correcting it when the riders started to overlap or flew too wide a pattern. So far, there were ten minor brushes, four wingtip burns, two bad collisions and two face-burnt riders. Wingtip injuries were just plain bad judgement. Collisions were caused by riders cutting it too fine and not staying focused. If this was a proper attack, then they would probably all be dead.

The Readers kept a tracking device on the dragons' responses, for no other creature could see such a distance in such detail. A human standing on the top of a mountain might see the vista but would never notice a lone wolf hunting, a slow-moving herd in a forest, or the movement of a rodent in the grass. Dragons could detect a beating heart or an injured prey from miles away, for their sense of smell was second to none, and it was this detailed information that poured back to the Readers so they could add the data to their findings.

The dragons were relentless and continued to destroy the targets with their flaming breath. What particles eluded the airborne beasts were efficiently seared into harmless ashes by the ground crew, or drawn into the trenches by the electromagnetic field around them.

*a *a *a

When all the targets had been eradicated, Sagitta glided towards the expanse of land that edged the sea and over the verdant softwoods that surrounded the northern shores. The Guardians didn't have their targets here and Bard leaned into the great neck, grasping the fighting straps firmly. Despite his weariness, he felt the sharp surge of elation which always gripped him when he flew on Sagitta. That merging of man and beast, brother with brother, air and wind, sun and fire. He always felt that Sagitta lived up to his nickname: Arrow—fast, immensely powerful, magnificently free. But he knew that Sagitta was distracted, knew what he was thinking—that the sea posed a serious problem if the hunters came that way, and there was a strong possibility that they would. The hunters were just as resourceful and opportunist as anyone else, so why had no one suggested practice sessions there? Sagitta dived into the water and Bard clung on tightly round his neck as they plunged to the bottom, skimmed along the seabed, then launched to the surface again. The sweat and soot had disappeared from both of them and Sagitta had found himself a tasty meal in the form of a giant squid.

'I will speak with Ser Alderman when we get back, we need to be prepared for a sea attack as well as on land. The riders will need to learn how to swim and how to stay underwater if need be.'

'The dragons as well!' Sagitta came back at him.

'I know, it's all very well being able to navigate in the sky and develop skills for an aerial ambush but the sea poses just as much a risk.'

'We can practice together,' came the message from Sagitta.

'Yes, we can, and we will do, but we have to get a team together so we know where the currents are and those dangerous rip tides. Even a dragon can drown if not sufficiently trained.'

As if to prove a point, Sagitta dipped his head into an arch and lurched forward again, which instinctively made Bard inhale a lungful of air.

You are a young dragon with way too much energy.

And you are a young man who has to train harder.

CHAPTER SIXTEEN

Bard slipped off Sagitta's back when they reached the palace.

'You go and find another meal for yourself and Bellatrix, we both know she won't have eaten. I need to go and speak with Ser Alderman about what we have seen.'

He knew that Sagitta had understood him when the dragon launched into the air without a second thought. He would be gone for some time. Time enough for Bard to air his concerns. Though when he got to Ser Alderman's quarters, he could hear a heated discussion from within.

'I tell you, they are getting closer.'

Bard knocked on the door and peeking his head round the edge saw the anxious face of Ijja.

'Come in, Bard, come in, You need to hear this.' Ser Alderman was in his chair watching Ijja pacing up and down the room.

'Is everything alright?'

'No, it isn't, Bard,' heralded an anxious Ijja. 'Everything is definitely not alright.'

Bard looked at Ser Alderman for clarification, his frown deepening with concern.

'Why don't you calm down and tell Bard what you have told me.'

'What? Again? I have already said what I found.'

'But I need you to tell Bard, as it will affect him as well.'

Ijja sighed heavily in protest and rolled his eyes.

'Ijja, whatever it is, we can't do anything tonight, it's pitch black out there.' Bard reminded him.

Ijja stared back at him for the longest time in response. 'All right, have it your way.'

Bard looked at Ser Alderman and breathed out heavily.

'I saw two dead dragons!' Ijja suddenly blurted out.

The shock announcement knocked Bard for six.

'What? When? Where?'

'I decided to go in another direction from everyone else, towards the mountains.'

They both looked at Ser Alderman, for it was forbidden after dusk.

'But it was a good thing that I did, because of what I found,' Ijja interjected at the look of concern.

'Near the mountains of Storma Bay?'

'Yes.'

'That's a long way.'

'I know, but I was keen to find something other than a practice target.'

'Is Bellatrix all right, that's a long way to take a dragon?'

'Why are you worrying about her when you should be paying attention to what I found?' Bard had to bite his bottom lip to stop the outburst. He knew he had probably pushed the dragon to exhaustion. He always did.

'What did you find?'

'Well, I was taking Bellatrix down so that she could have a rest. We had been flying for some time and I knew she was getting cold.'

Bard nodded his head, already detecting the lie.

'She landed on some soft snow in a glen. I got off to have a look around. I left her to rest and that's when I saw the footprints.'

'Dragon footprints?'

'No, imbecile, listen!'

Bard breathed deeply and pursed his lips. Ser Alderman extended his hand for Ijja to continue.

'I saw the remains of a fire sticking out through the fallen snow, and when I looked up, that's when I saw the dragon. I told Bellatrix to stay where she was while I investigated—I didn't want her to get frightened.' He aimed that last bit at Ser Alderman who nodded his head in gratitude. 'It was in a terrible state, first being brought down by an arrow poisoned with tar and sulphur, then all its scales cruelly cut away. It was horrible.' Ijja pulled a face and shook his head.

'How did you know it was tar and sulphur?' Bard queried.

'Because of the smell, and I could see that the creature had burns from the inside out.'

Bard sniffed away a runny nose and tried to compose himself. 'Anything else?'

'Yes, another dragon had been brought down in the same way. That one was dead on the ground.'

'The hunters are close then?'

'Yes, I believe so.'

'What shall we do, Ser Alderman?'

'I will need to get the council together to see what is the best way forward.'

'We don't have time for that,' butted in Ijja.

Ser Alderman glared at him. 'Ijja, you have been

very good in bringing this to my attention. Yes, what you did was wrong, in taking a dragon so far out that you put both your lives in danger. You were lucky that she wasn't brought down by the hunters as well. Nevertheless, I cannot make a decision without the input of the council.'

'But—'

'There's no buts, Ijja. We have time on our side and I am obligated to get consent from my Officials and the Grandmaster about such an important matter. Is that clear?'

Ijja nodded meekly.

Bard waited for the tension to subside before he spoke up. 'May I make a suggestion, Ser Alderman?'

'Please do.'

'I came to see you today primarily for something I had noticed as well.'

Ijja looked up in surprise, concerned that his news may be surpassed by something more momentous.

'I was flying over the sea today, and realised it could possibly be another route for the hunters to attack.'

Ijja breathed a sigh of relief and tittered behind a fake cough as Bard continued.

'I also wondered if we should get the dragons and their riders used to the vast expanse of water. Perhaps diving deep into the sea and becoming familiar with the conditions?'

Something that little kids should be doing, Ijja thought. Nothing can beat my revelation.

'Perhaps if Ijja and myself were to go out tomorrow morning, we could survey it together ?'

'I think that's an excellent idea, Bard. What say you to that, Ijja?'

Ijja nodded his head. 'Well, I can't see us being attacked by flaming arrows of tar and sulphur, so I think it's a great idea.'

'Early tomorrow morning?'

'Yes, let's go at sunrise.'

'No heroics mind you. This is an observation session only.'

'Of course,' smiled Ijja. 'When have I ever been anything other than responsible?'

CHAPTER SEVENTEEN

Sagitta liked the rough hills that bordered the complex. He was adept at following the markers of the land in flight. He glided close to the ground, sometimes barely skimming the mottled flora that cloaked the rocky hills. When his red wings moved, it was an almost effortless motion that matched the gigantic shadow beneath him. He was hunting.

The two dragons flew close together and despite their size were still able to dive down and take an unsuspecting animal without being detected. Bellatrix followed his lead and was becoming as adept as he was. She caught the pungent aroma of deer grazing peacefully in the brilliant sunshine, flicking away nuisance flies; the stags supporting their heavy racks of antlers. Those protruding bones could inflict a lot of damage on a dragon, so she focused on a small female that was straying from the rest of the herd. Foolish decision she thought, always stay together, for even a dragon, on their own, is a prime target. The doe startled—suddenly, losing her footing as she turned, frantically searching out the alpha male to come to her aid, but he was hidden as the other does bolted around him. The noise was of chaos, terror, and a stampeding herd fleeing for their lives. The alpha stopped to look for her, but it was too late. In a frantic dive, the front talons seized the doe and held it close to the keel of her chest. The doe struggled briefly, spattering blood everywhere but her heart gave out before she was ripped to pieces. The stag lifted his head to smell the blood. That panicked him so he moved on—quickly. Still, he looked back just once to make sure, but seeing the dragon consuming every part of the doe's body, he knew there was nothing he could do. He followed the rest of the herd into the canopy of the forest, where they would be safe—for the time being at least.

Sagitta landed next to Bellatrix, his golden talons tipped in blood.

There is good feeding to be had here.

There really is, and we are so lucky to have this around us.

We are lucky to have each other, Bella.

You are what keeps me going, Sagitta. When that wretched collar is tight around my throat, I have to think of you to stop myself from giving up.

But it's not on all the time now, the Guardians made Ijja remove it.

No, it's not, and I know have the other Tribunes to thank for that, but Ijja still puts it on when he thinks that no one is looking.

You must never give up. Never let him think that he has won, or that he has crushed you. It will make him worse.

They rubbed their muzzles together.

Come, we have to get back to the complex. Bard has asked for an early start.

I don't think I have the energy today. I flew so far yesterday.

I know, but you have fed well this morning, so that should give you added strength. I will watch out for you.

They nuzzled again and took to the air.

ཻ ཻ ཻ

Bard and Ijja had risen with the sun and were surveying the tranquil waters in front of them. The early morning was the best time for seeing the strange creatures of the deep oceans; many a boy had boasted about seeing a whale breach, or a pod of dolphins at play. Seals would bask in the sunlight, and turtles would come ashore at this time.

Of course, Ijja had swum with one, or so he said. 'It was so large that it carried me out to sea.'

'Really?'

'Yes, really, I've swum with them all; large ones, small ones, brown ones, green ones, black ones.'

'Do they mind you riding them?'

'No, not at all. It's funny to watch them come ashore carrying their cumbersome load and struggling in the sand. But when you swim with them in the sea then they are as nimble as a water nymph or a weight-less moon—they own the sea.'

'You are very lucky.'

'I know I'm lucky to have had the opportunity to ride such an incredible creature, so much better than this thing I am lumbered with now.'

Bard saw Bellatrix drop her head low, she knew when Ijja was ridiculing her.

'But now is the best time for seeing them,' Ijja continued. 'During the day they swim deep or hide in crevasses, but when the sun is newly risen, that's when they come to the surface.'

❧ ❧ ❧

To the east, the first pale light of day permeated the sky above the water. The clouds in the sky were aglow at this time: pink, crimson, maroon and gold.

'That looks like you,' Bard said to Sagitta. 'Those amazing colours have morphed into a red dragon with wings.'

Bard felt the contentment of Sagitta looking up into the sky and enjoying the first rays of sunlight on his skin. Then came the soft swish of waves. The great ball in the sky poured energy over the tides and illuminated the white surf on the crest of a wave. Bard sat astride Sagitta and watched the sun bounce off the crystal waters in front of him, merging with the specks of nothing on a distant skyline. Since being here, he had come to appreciate the sharp salty smell of the air and the vastness of the horizon trimmed with a band of azure on a clear day, while the sea remained a rich shade of cyan.

He guided Sagitta into action to ride the waves and felt the heat on their backs from the intense golden sun. He looked over to Ijja who was brutally digging his heels into Bellatrix, trying to get her into the air, but she wasn't ready for this kind of exertion—she was still recovering from the exhausting flight the previous day.

'She's all right,' argued Ijja when Bard suggested he

took another dragon out. 'She's young and energetic, she can handle it.'

But Bellatrix's austere composure suggested anything but youth and vitality. With a yank on the reins and a powerful kick into her side, he got her into the air. He was yelling at her continually to go faster over the waves and find the turtles.

Then suddenly, and without any warning, the weather changed.

The mist came first. It closed in wet and heavy, obscuring the cliffs and then the sky itself. A cloud of granite thundered past, the waves turned tempestuous and angry. Bard could see little and the sound of crashing waves filled his ears. Then a movement beneath the sea told him that something unnatural was very close.

Under the waves, Bard could see ominous shapes and dark sea creatures swimming in the water below him. Then a large thump shuddered against the seabed and sent a mini tidal wave from below. Bard looked through the mist for Ijja but he was too far out to sea now and probably wasn't aware of what was happening around him.

Ijja, unperturbed and unaffected by the change in his environment, continued to dive into the water and rise out like a dart—deaf and blind to his surroundings and the safety of his dragon. Bellatrix did everything she could to please her master. Despite her increasing fatigue, she did not want the collar back on. Ijja waved to Bard, beckoning him to follow, though when Bard ignored him and kept Sagitta back, he came closer to the shore, and began calling him a coward.

Suddenly, the mountain of a sea serpent's body rose from the waves. Bard held Sagitta back and channelled his message to not go in and fight. Sagitta heeded the warning, but Ijja did not.

'Leave it,' cried out Bard. 'We have come onto its territory. It's only defending itself.' 'Have you not heard of the sea monster that devours humans?' Ijja retorted brazenly.

'Do not take Bellatrix that way, come full circle to avoid the beast.'

'Not a chance,' shouted back Ijja. 'If we can make these waters safe by ridding them of this creature, then we can protect everyone.'

'But if we leave the monster where it is, then it will do the job for us, don't you see?'

'If you are scared, Bard, then turn back. I am going to prove to everyone how courageous I am.'

'This is no time for heroics, Ijja, we have been told to not take chances when practising. We should only stick to the allocated training grounds. Besides, Bellatrix is not strong enough.'

'Of course she is. She is a dragon, and this is the perfect opportunity for her to show me how capable she really is.'

'No...' But Bard's instructions got lost on the breeze and Ijja took his dragon ever closer to the enormous reptilian body. The huge thing reeled around them with such speed that the armoured scales —each the size of a mainsail—were a blur. The spray and ripple of the serpent soaked the dragon and its rider. The noise was deafening. Bard kept Sagitta back.

Ijja wrestled with the reins as he guided his dragon ever closer, his muscles and veins stood out like banners as he cruised alongside the serpent, riding the currents in the amphibian's direction. He had seen this creature once before when he was riding the back of a turtle. Hydra, the hideous monster with six eyes on six long snaky necks, each one equipped with a massive head containing three rows of yellow serrated teeth. Her body consisted of twelve tentacle-like arms and a long viper's tail, while an assortment of weapons fringed her waist. In this form she attacked the ships of passing sailors, for their figurehead was always a female—and Hydra hated females.

'Now, we'll see what you are made of you pathetic dragon!' Ijja drove Bellatrix even closer.

Hydra's necks were longer than any ship's masts. Her six heads were hideously lumpy and misshapen, like blocks of melted lava stone. Black tongues flicked from the orifice and licked her sword-like teeth, caressing the remains of rotting flesh with pungent-smelling drool.

Her necks began to ripple and she screamed her attack call, a piercing chaotic pitch, and from one of her mouths, a gleaming strand of saliva trailed as the monster dived towards Bellatrix. The dragon felt the monstrous tentacles trying to grab her, turning her and spinning her in the air. Ijja felt the monster's wrath as his shoulder collided with a talon, and feeling the bruise emerge under the pain he was thankful for a bruise rather than a break.

'You stupid dragon, get me out of here,' he cussed, holding on as tight as he could but it wasn't tight enough and he felt himself falling. 'Damn you, Bellatrix, when I get out of this I will throttle you with that collar until you are begging for your life.'

Bellatrix opened her eyes to search for Ijja as she was tossed between the rotating arms. She reached down to him, extending one of her free talons to catch him. She breathed a sigh of relief when his jacket suddenly pointed upwards—she had caught him. He was spinning on a few threads as the creature went in for the attack. But it wasn't Bellatrix that had him, it was the serpent.

She saw him draw a breath of air as the surface of the water came up to meet him, but it was too late. He smashed into the sea, sucking water into his lungs moments before one of the arms lifted him high, and put him whole into a wide open mouth.

The dragon writhed frantically, gasping for air as Hydra gripped her by the throat with another arm; the sound of tearing flesh was unbearable. Bellatrix screamed fire, her tail lashed from side to side, but the monstrous Hydra was not about to give up. For the once beautiful Hydra had been poisoned by a jealous rival and turned into a monster so hideous, that now, any female form was seen as the enemy.

Sagitta roared and dove towards the creature. Hydra shook Bellatrix with one of her heads before tackling the male. The other heads whipped and struck his body, but he was twice her size and Hydra had met her match, yet still, her cobra necks were thrashing back and forth determined to tear him limb from limb, snapping her huge jaws around anything they could find. Sagitta breathed fire over the huge body while Bard, in range, quickly strung a bow and fired into one of the mouths, but with Bellatrix firmly held in one, there were still four more to deal with.

Bellatrix was limp and lifeless now, her eyes shut tight while her body was thrown around like a child's toy.

Then, out of the clouds above her, another female dragon, with wings folded back like a dart, dived down with her tribune gripping on for dear life. Receiving a distress call from her younger sibling, Pyxis was furiously trying to send a message back but knew it wasn't getting through. The sun turned her wings golden, and as the light flashed in Hydra's eyes, another head screamed in protest exposing the razor-sharp teeth, but instead of retreating, Pyxis dived at the monster, her body tensed for combat. Sagitta launched in while Hydra was occupied with the advancing female, opening his jaws wide and ripping off one of the heads leaving tendons and sinew trailing as he spat it out into the sea. The talons of the advancing dragon ripped into Hydra's flank and she screamed in agony. With desperation born of panic, Bellatrix wrenched herself free, her huge talons leaving gouges to the bone along the monster's shoulders. Then, beating for altitude she slashed at one of Hydra's heads and took out an eye. Hydra's tortured scream sent shock waves across the ocean, and another tentacle grabbed at Bellatrix's wing, the claws dragging through the muscles, pulling her wing from its socket. Pyxis breathed fire into the monster's wounds, and as Hydra writhed and screamed, Bellatrix was able to get away. But she couldn't fly. She was falling. Sagitta flew in quickly, his wings out wide and caught Bellatrix in his talons before she could plunge into the sea. Bellatrix hissed, craning her neck, this way and that, and while her head, reflected in the water showed her incredulity, horror, and pain, her body was seized with a massive convulsion. Sagitta held onto her tightly. She let out a scream. They were nearly at the shore, and as Sagitta laid her gently on the warm sand, her eyes closed, her body sagged, and her breathing slowed. He nuzzled her with his snout, a single tear falling into each eye. She opened one and he saw his reflection; she was severely wounded, but she would not die. He told her what he saw. He nuzzled her again but he had to go and help Pyxis. Leaving her on the shoreline he veered round to attack once more but saw Pyxis's rider fall as the long arm of a tentacle knocked him from his mount. The female roared in response and dove down to save her tribune, but the sound of Haynes' back breaking as he hit the water meant another rider was lost to the sea. Pyxis roared and sank her teeth into Hydra's skin, her talons digging deeply into her back, her jaws sinking into the unprotected neck, and with a mighty rip, a major artery was severed. She snapped again, taking an arm, and another, and another. Bard was able to home in on his target as Sagitta came round again. This time he released six arrows in quick succession and blood spurted from the bulbous eyes. The dragons circled the stricken monster breathing fire onto every flailing limb as Bard sank arrow after arrow into the heaving mass of blubber. The monster stopped her fight. She couldn't see, and all her limbs had been severed or lacerated to the extent that they were numb and useless. With life oozing from the puncture wounds, she lost her strength and slowly disappeared into the depths of the sea. And only when the bubbles stopped coming to the surface did they know the mighty Hydra was dead.

Sagitta and Pyxis stayed with Bellatrix as Bard raced up the incline to the complex above. Taking three steps at a time and brushing aside the safety rope, he kept his eyes fixed on the high walls and domes of the great Dragon Palace above. Entering the postern gate, he strode past the Officials, through the passageways and pounded down the walkways in long strides that shook the bones of everyone he passed. Once at the observation tower he made his way to the platform where the Officials had congregated. Ser Alderman's austere command stopped him in his tracks. 'Is there something wrong, Bard?'

'Something wrong? Did no one think to tell us there was a hideous monster that lived *out there* in the sea?'

Ser Alderman looked through the window, the Grandmaster was hidden in a veiled chair looking through a slender telescope.

'Ser Alderman… did you know?'

Ser Alderman continued to look out of the window with his hands clenched tight behind his back. 'Yes, Bard, we knew.'

'Then why did no one tell us?'

Ser Alderman spun around.

'Because Ijja was a fool. He had learned nothing in his years here, and his reckless behaviour would have caused the death of every tribune that we have, not to mention the poor dragon he delighted in torturing on a daily basis. He had to go; and when you said about the sea, I had no choice, I knew he would be foolhardy.'

'Ser Alderman…' Bard tried to curtail his emotion. 'I understand your anger and frustration, but we lost Haynes as well, and Bellatrix is severely wounded. Sagitta and Pyxis are with her now.'

'There will always be casualties in war.'

'But we're not at war.'

'Oh yes, we are.'

Ser Alderman snapped his fingers and a team of Guardians went to get Bellatrix and prepare her for surgery.

'Ijja knew about Hydra.'

Ser Alderman and Bard looked towards the disembodied voice as a ray of light lit up the Grandmaster's chair.

'He knew?'

'Yes, he knew.' Came the ethereal voice.

'How did he know?'

'Because I saw him researching it in the library.'

Bard was speechless. Ser Alderman turned crimson with anger. The Grandmaster leaned back in the chair and whispered again.

'He ran into the library one day, excited that he had ridden a turtle. He was ecstatic and shouting it out to everyone and anyone. I was incensed that he had so little regard for those around him who were busy researching and quietly reading but the stillness enabled me to listen in further. I heard the librarian warning him about Hydra, that she was a hideous monster concealed within the depths of the ocean after a curse had been placed on her. Of course, he laughed at the librarian—like he always does—*did…* but I heard the librarian warning him not to take Bellatrix there because it was a female who cursed her, and that Hydra would most certainly seek retribution.'

'He did it deliberately then?' Bard's voice was quiet in the consuming revelation. 'He deliberately wanted to frighten Bellatrix or even get her killed.'

Ser Alderman was grinding his teeth. 'I'd prefer to think that Hydra despises foolhardy individuals and it was *he* that she was after.'

Bard nodded. 'She's dead now though.'

'Don't be too sure, Bard. Hydra has survived for centuries down there. Some say she comes back bigger and more brutal after each encounter.' The Grand-master sank back into the chair as a cloud came in front of the sun and blocked Bard's view.

'I have scheduled a council meeting.' Ser Alderman broke the silence.

'When for?' interjected Bard.

'Tomorrow morning.'

CHAPTER EIGHTEEN

The Council Room was the size of a cathedral, the towering roof supported by a forest of white columns. High arched windows opened onto broad balconies that overlooked the kingdom. A rainbow of tapestries covered the walls, embroidered with scenes of the Imperial Dragon's long reign. On one tapestry stood the Queen of Dragons posing in triumph on a golden gilded column. Her consort, the duke, was on the other. While the tapestries caught the eye with their bright colours and exquisite detail, the most arresting feature of the room was the polished marble floor; inlaid with coloured stone, precious metals, and gems that morphed into an elaborate map of the dragon kingdoms. Ser Alderman studied the map with the council, finding the jagged contours, the wide oceans and huge expanse of nothing that covered a thousand miles in length. It showed all the kingdoms the dragons had once owned, and now he feared that the hunters had somehow got hold of this information. There were two kingdoms north of Bergen. One was Storma Bay: a land of immense rivers and trackless deserts, endless forests and jagged mountains. This was where Bellatrix had stopped to rest and found the carcasses of two Mountain Dragons. The other kingdom was a vast, isolated and impenetrable land of ice, populated by the third species, the Ice Dragons who made their home in the Ice Palace of Boreas Crown; a mountain range so remote, with dragons so large, that they made the Lowland Dragons look like wild dogs with wings. He doubted very much if the hunters would venture that far north, which left the Lowland Dragons of Bergen next on the list. He breathed in deeply as the awful reality sank in.

Far across the room, hidden from view, the Grandmaster sat sipping on a double measure of the finest cognac and listened to their mumblings with interest. The conversation between the Alderman and the councillors piqued the Grandmaster's interest and a gloved hand summoned Ser Alderman over. An exchange of whispers followed, after which Ser Alderman gave voice to the exchange.

'Our Grandmaster has said that we will need to evacuate everyone to the Ice Palace of Boreas Crown.'

The councillors looked aghast.

'That's our very last resort,' said the Reader. 'It's the furthest north, and not all the dragons would make it. We don't want them running out of steam like Bellatrix did at Storma Bay, and landing where the hunters have their camp.'

The Grandmaster whispered in a hoarse voice. 'I still think we should start to evacuate now—to save everyone.'

Ser Alderman interjected. 'I'm going to send a search party out. We need to determine if the hunters are coming this way or venturing further north. It's unlikely that they are heading towards Boreas Crown because of the difficult terrain, but we have no way of knowing. Where Bellatrix found the dead dragons is midway between the Lowland Dragons and the Ice Dragons, so we know they are heading for one of us.'

'I see the dilemma,' whispered the Grandmaster in the deep gravelly voice. 'Yes, we will be safer with the Ice Dragons, their size and numbers will be protection enough, but we are likely to lose a good few of our own if we undertake the perilous journey.'

'Exactly, they will be picked off like flies. These

hunters are experts now. They know what they are doing.'

'But the dragons are the masters of the earth, millions of years of evolution have produced dragons as the highest form of life.'

Everyone looked at the Guardian who had spoken with such passion; no one wanted to disillusion him. A voice from one of the Officials came from the back.

'Many years ago that was true, but now, the dragons can only be certain of safety when all the hunters are dead, and the best way to do that is on our own territory. Here, we know the lie of the land, the contours of the hills and the face of the cliffs. Going to the mountains has to be the very last option, the very last.'

'The Tribunes will be here soon, it has to be their decision as well,' Fellow135 spoke up. The Grandmaster nodded and whispered. 'Of course, but I fear we are running out of time.'

A noise along the hallway told the council that the Tribunes were approaching. The Grandmaster disappeared behind the veil and waited silently for the Tribunes to take their seats and for Ser Alderman to begin the proceedings.

🐾 🐾 🐾

'I asked all of you here because we need to talk about yesterday's events as well as some new developments. But first, Bard, how is Bellatrix?'

'She is resting in the infirmary, thanks to the quick actions of Sagitta and Pyxis.'

'Good, which is more than can be said of Ijja, too hot-headed for his own good.'

Bard's solemn expression remained and he shook his head slowly from side to side as he recalled Ijja's last few moments.

'You are too kind, Bard, but that boy would have killed anyone that flew with him. He was a liability. You know that, I know that, everyone knows that.'

Bard knew that it was all planned and suddenly came to his senses as Ser Alderman was still talking.

'Mind you take no blame. We are lucky that Bellatrix still lives, she is the important one here.'

'Lives, yes, but probably won't be able to fly again.'

The air hung heavy with remorse for the dragon and for the death of Tribune Haynes.

Ser Alderman pursed his lips, desperately trying to form some words of positivity in such a grave situation. But he couldn't. Instead, he nodded a bit, mumbled something to the Grandmaster, and nodded some more before he turned his attention to the matter he had gathered everyone for.

'Our prayers are with the deceased. We will learn from these mistakes. But right now, we need to get a flight team to cover the mountains. The hunters have been spotted and we need to gather evidence to determine how fast they are travelling and if they are coming this way.' 'What do we do if they are coming this way?'

'We have to be battle ready.'

'But if they *are* the hunters then they will become aware of our dragons while we are tracking them,' said Ramou.

'Not if the dragons fly high enough and each rider carries a tracking device.'

'We would have to fly when it is cloudy,' said Bard. 'A clear sky would make the dragons too conspicuous.'

Tribune Dram was nodding his head in unconscious agreement. 'Because we have already lost two Tribunes, we need more riders and dragons to search the terrain, even if it means the high ranking Officials joining us.'

The Grandmaster leaned forward from the shadows, coughed a bit, and then whispered. 'How does everyone feel about that?'

'*All* of the Officials flying with the Tribunes?' asked the Imperial Herald.

'Is that a problem?' came the response from Dram.

The unexpected notion sent a murmurous ripple through the meeting as the Grandmaster motioned for calm. 'What does everyone say to that?'

The Guardian of the Dragons rose, glanced at the Sword-master, and ticked his head. 'We should *all* ride, every one of us. If we have to defend the dragons' palace and everyone in it, then *all* of us have to play our part.'

'But what if we are *all* slaughtered?'

The sword-master span round to face Tribune Davio. 'The hunters will slaughter everyone, regardless of whether they ride a dragon or not. These murderers do not see what is at stake if they do not control their avarice. Death comes to everyone unless they play their part in protecting what we have.'

His words left a bitter aftertaste as each person digested the terrible consequences.

Bard broke the silence. 'We should mount an expedition to fly at dawn; the clouds will be low and we will be camouflaged.' He saw Ramou and Alto nodding their heads in agreement, but noticed the Imperial Herald bristle, he hadn't flown a dragon for many years and was understandably concerned. But he had the attention of Ser Reader. He spoke quickly and clearly. 'Ser Reader, you have knowledge of the mountain range, could you describe the land to us. Would you say that we had to cover an area as large as several constellations?'

Ser Reader nodded his head. 'With the number of riders that you are talking about we could divide the area up into sections. The Tribunes cover the farthest area, the Officials will decide among themselves who covers what is left. I can gather maps and other data to show you all what the terrain is like in each section.'

Ser Alderman had been listening intently, and when everyone had spoken, he aired his findings on the matter. 'Tribune Davio is correct, if all of us go, then the palace is unprotected and vulnerable. I could not allow such an expedition now that I have heard what is involved. I hope you agree with me that it is far more important to protect what we have. I can assure you that once we are able to determine some coordinates acceptable to both riders and dragons, we can send a volunteer group to explore the terrain. I know how much territory one dragon can cover, and all of the Officials have vital information that they can feed to the Tribunes.'

The Grandmaster summoned Ser Alderman with an outstretched finger and spent a considerable time in an exchange of whispers and head shaking. Eventually, Ser Alderman stood up and bowed to the Grandmaster before facing the group. 'The Grandmaster and

I have reached an agreement. We would rather work on the skills and techniques that we have already developed, and let the Tribunes and their dragons use what they have learned.' There was a ripple of assent. 'The Grandmaster agrees that we work together, using the knowledge that we have become proficient in, knowing that each of us needs the expertise of another to survive.' He had to stop because everyone was now cheering and embracing in unity. The Imperial Herald breathed out a sigh of relief. Ser Reader wiped his brow.

'We will send out a search party in three days. Tribunes, make sure that you rest and eat during that time. We don't want to see anyone flying or practising combat before then. Guardians, see to all the dragons' needs; feeding, oiling, scrubbing, cleaning. Temple boys, you answer to your Guardian. Ser Reader, I want those telescopes polished and prepped and in full working order, and Ser Herald, you work on the radar and transmissions with your orderlies. The Grandmaster will be following the events from the Grand Room in the master apartments. I will be on hand to help Ser Reader and Ser Herald with any technical problems, if and when they arise. Now, everyone, as we have a very important assignment to complete, go to your stations and prepare.

CHAPTER NINETEEN

On the western side of the complex, beneath the ground floor apartments, a winding maze of chambers led to the infirmary. Here, the air smelled of paper and dust and years gone by. Around the expanse, wooden shelves rose high into the dimness, crammed with leather-bound books and boxes of ancient scrolls. The vast chamber was a library of information on anatomy and physiology including detailed anatomy structure, skeletal development, brain function, seizures, remedies, muscle formation, growth, repair, and development—all for dragons. Between the rows of books were hundreds of shelves filled with handblown vials of all sizes and shapes, their healing contents gleaming in the light of the small window slits that lined the chamber. The Physician sat at a desk in the middle of the labyrinth, a massive tome open before him, the pages bearing colourful detailed drawings of the inner workings of a dragon's wing. His hair hung long past his shoulders and a beard trailed even longer and whiter. Spectacles balanced on the bridge of his nose, and despite his ageing years, no one knew the anatomy of a dragon better than the Physician.

Bellatrix was still asleep. The ground lay beneath her, swirling, spinning, swimming in colours. A heavy weight pressed against her stomach and she remembered she was falling. She recalled bracing for impact, but the wind wasn't brushing against her face now. The seconds it should take her to reach the ground had passed. She opened her eyes, blinking to clear her vision. Forgetting where she was, her eyes flared in panic, but then she felt the familiar presence of the two dragons she loved the most; Sagitta and her sister.

Sagitta lay beside her. Bellatrix had been so still he'd wondered if she was dead. He looked for the movement of her chest, rising and falling, and that gave him the reassurance that he needed, but her wing was a mass of patches, stitches, and bloodstains; it looked like it would never heal at all.

As her eyes began to focus, her mind rose through the pain in her body. Then, as she gathered what strength remained, the muscles convulsed and she screamed out loud. 'SAGITTA!'

Bellatrix woke to confusion. For three days she'd tossed and turned, the horrors of that dreadful morning consuming her every being. The smell of lavender hung in the air, with a touch of camomile and camphor. The ambient temperature was moist and warm, aiding the healing of her injuries. She saw the Guardians preparing a potion for her to drink.

'Here have this.' The Guardian knew she was disorientated. 'You are in the infirmary. You are safe now. And your friends have been with you all the time.' He smiled at the two dragons and went back to preparing lotions and potions and getting more cleaning materials together. Sagitta moved closer when she called his name.

He nuzzled Bellatrix' head with his own and closed his eyes, concentrating. The tiny machines that swam in Bellatrix were controlled by her mental commands. If she had lost consciousness before willing the molecular cells to heal her, they wouldn't do so, and that's what he was afraid of. But Sagitta had the skills needed to mend damaged tissue, to knit together once more the ruptured blood vessels. He couldn't bear to lose her.

'Give me a knife,' he said to Pyxis. Pyxis handed

him a blade, shining and sharp. 'What are you doing?' she asked.

'Just keep your eyes on Bella.' He cut a gash across his front foot, releasing a ribbon of red. He took Bella's, and did the same, then placed both their pads together.

'Do your job,' he whispered. 'Heal her.' With great concentration, he guided the active cells into Bella's blood. He told the cells to multiply, which they did. As they multiplied and spread, he blocked out the distractions in the infirmary, listening only to the reports of the microscopic warriors in Bella's body, plotting, in his mind's eye, a map of Bella's wounds. After a little while, he could see the extent of her injuries as if his eyes could see right through her muscles and layers of cartilage. He willed the cells to knit her ruptured vessels back together, and they obeyed. He found a bit of cartilage resistant to the healing cells, so he sent more messages to the tiny warriors to fix the strands and put it all back together. There was too much adrenaline around her heart, so he sent messages to the liver and kidneys to remove the blocking agents. He was aware of every intricate movement, of every healing warrior cell doing its job. He felt her heart returning to normal, her breathing became less laboured, he even saw a twinge of the injured wing as it knitted and wove life-saving strands into the muscles. He could see inside her mind and saw the pain was subsiding. He felt her strength returning along with her will to live. She was more relaxed and less afraid now.

Sagitta, are you there?

I'm here, Bella, I'm here right by your side. You are safe.

She opened one eye, then the other, and breathed out a happy sigh when she saw him.

I'm so glad to see you awake at last, I feared you would die.

You told me never to give up, so I didn't.

Sagitta nuzzled her. *My strong girl.*

Are you all right? Did you get hurt? she asked him.

No, and neither did Pyxis, she has been here as well.

Thank you for saving me.

We both love you, Bellatrix, said Pyxis, *and we are so happy to see you awake.*

I can't move much, it's still a bit sore.

It will take time, the worst is over, now you must rest. Sagitta's voice was full of reassurance.

I sense that you have to go now, Sagitta, I can feel that something quite urgent awaits.

Yes, said Sagitta, *we have an assignment to track the hunters.*

Please be careful, I had a dream about Bard and a dead

dragon. A great beast, huge, with wings so large they would cover this palace. The beast had fallen on top of Bard, but Bard was alive and the dragon was dead.

It was only a dream, dear one, I will be careful and take care of him.

And take care of yourself, I feel evil at work. Her tone of concern continued.

Everything will be fine, Bella. Don't you worry. It's more important that you rest.

I know what you have just done for me, Sagitta.

He nuzzled her again. *You will get strong now, maybe even stronger than before, and as soon as I get back, I will come and see you.*

I will be here, in the same place, with my sister at my side.

Their necks entwined in a fond farewell, and Sagitta went off to prepare for the mission.

CHAPTER TWENTY

Now they had shared each other's blood, they had a greater bond and closeness. He had given her the power to mend her own wing, and for that, she would be eternally grateful—he knew that. But there was. Occasionally, he had found this particular closeness distracting, especially over the past few days when he had been preparing for this long flight, but mostly it was the most wonderful feeling he had ever experienced, a feeling that had ignited a desire to protect her at all costs—to be with her no matter what. He stood, blinking at the day around him, feeling as though he had just been awakened. The other dragons and their Tribunes were gathered together outside the complex.

He would be flying with Dram and Lacerta. Fortunately, he and Lacerta had feasted early that morning, so they had enough energy for the long flight ahead, and after the feat he had just pulled off he needed all the energy he could muster. Bard was waiting with Dram, ready to mount their dragons. Lacerta snapped his wings wide open, and as they cracked into motion he reared up on his hind legs and roared.

Lacerta is in a feisty mood today, Bard.

Yes, I can see that, but you just take it easy today, brother.

I will because I have someone very important waiting for my return.

Bard smiled at the blossoming love between the two dragons and climbed into position. He adjusted his tracking device. 'Are you ready, Dram? Can you hear me?'

With that question barely past Bard's lips, Lacerta suddenly brushed past them both leaving a strong breeze in a chaotic swirl and a small patch of soil in a frenzy. Sagitta did not hesitate to follow and launched himself into the air, his powerful body undulating like a serpent as he fought his way higher into the sky. His wings created a slow throb in the air with every pull followed by a deep grunting sound as he nestled into the flight path.

The stone walls of the palace were minute specks within minutes as Sagitta veered upwards. They were flying high above the forest in no time. In the distance, they could see the gleaming silver ribbon of the river. They soared into the clouds where they would be safe from prying eyes. Here, the wind got colder, and tiny particles of ice drifted and shimmered in the brilliant sunlight so that they seemed to be journeying through a world of polished crystal. Bard leaned into Sagitta to stay warm, while the glittering white world rolled rapidly past.

It was a long flight, the most direct route from the peninsular of Bergen to the mountains of Storma Bay. The huge dragon soared, catching the prevailing wind and, with great sweeps of his wings, sped through the cooler air, high above the mountainous terrain. As Sagitta settled down to long-distance flying, Bard had much to do. With the tracking device bleeping and the dragon's eye for detail, he had noticed the ground changing with evidence of human life, of groups, of food and fires and weapon making.

The sun was low over the mountains to the west as the convoy spread over the valley.

By now Bard was far beyond the river. Sagitta was a swift and powerful flyer; miles could pass during a moment lost to thought. It did him good to fly like this. But he needed to keep his wits about him and stay on high alert. Bard looked to the left to search for the pole star that Ser Reader had plotted, but he couldn't see it. He started as he realised that Lacerta, one of the biggest dragons was flying directly above him and blocking his view. He signalled to Lacerta to keep in line, but Lacerta was being guided by Dram into a collision course. Bard pulled up hard to avoid the collision and shouted at him. 'What are you doing?'

Dram was signalling to him.

'What's going on?' said Bard again. 'Is there something wrong?'

Dram drove hard at him again. Bard had no alternative but to switch the frequency on the tracking device so those at the observation tower could hear the problem. 'I'm in trouble here, or Dram seems to be in trouble, I'm not sure which.'

There was a crackle of lines as Ser Reader asked him to repeat.

'I'm in trouble.' Bard tried to give the coordinates but the huge dragon kept butting into them.

Sagitta craned his neck around to see what was happening. He felt the urgency in Bard's voice and pumped his wings furiously. Bard clung on, crouching down over his neck, moving with the force of the dragon. He looked down and saw the broad expanse of

Storma Bay looming up below. Lacerta continued to ram into them, guided by Dram.

'Sagitta, something is wrong, Dram is urging us to land. We have to get over that ridge.'

Sagitta sped up, his speed and agility giving him an advantage but Lacerta passed beneath him with nothing to spare. Without warning, something snaked through the air with a snap and impaled itself in Bard's leg. Searing pain flashed up his spine before he was able to pull it out. He clung on for dear life as he felt himself losing consciousness. Sagitta knew of the danger Bard was in and tried to slow down, but Lacerta came at him again and rammed into his side. Sagitta started to plummet. He was receiving no messages from Bard now, he had to land soon or risk Bard falling to his death. He was skimming across the treetops, layers of snow tumbling to the ground as he flew past. The branches snatched and dragged at him, yanking him into the canopy. Bard was thrown some distance as Sagitta crashed onto the soft snow and lay there, stunned, all breath knocked from his body until sharp claws wrapped themselves in the fringe of scales along his skull and jerked his head back. A blade cut into his throat.

'What are you doing?' Sagitta communicated through thought.

'Dram is my master and I have to do as I am told.'

'Do as you are told, what exactly does that mean?'

'I have to report back that there have been no sightings of the hunters.'

'Why?'

'Because Dram is one of them. He has been feeding them information about the dragons for several days now.'

'What? No, surely not.'

'It's true.'

'And you would betray your own kind, for a hunter?'

'He is my master first, hunter second. I have to obey him.'

'So what are you going to do with us?'

'We will have to kill you both.'

'But the Officials will think it was the hunters and prepare everyone for battle.'

'No, they won't, because Dram will tell them there was an accident.'

'I can't believe this. So what is Dram getting out of it?'

'Money of course. Something happened back at Aiden Hall where his father was a farmhand. I think he made a young girl pregnant and was ordered off the land. But he has been planning this attack for several days, ever since Ijja made the discovery, and he will make his fortune from this alliance.'

'Where is he now?'

'He is leaving a sign for the hunters. How far away the palace is and when the best time to attack is.'

'And you've gone along with all of this and not said a word to anyone. Bard could have died back there. Have you no honour?'

'You talk about honour! I've been stuck at that palace for years. I am a prisoner there. You have only just arrived, you have no idea what it's like.'

'You can leave at any time, Lacerta, why don't you simply fly off? The Officials always say that the dragons are not prisoners.'

'Dram owns me. He has always owned me and that binds us. Though now he has promised my freedom in return for my loyalty.'

Sagitta thought of Bellatrix and how she'd stayed loyal to Ijja despite the cruelty, and now Lacerta was prepared to betray his friends to the enemy.

'I don't understand this; you would betray us to the hunters for your freedom?'

'Yes.'

Sagitta had heard enough. He jerked his head backwards, slamming into Lacerta's snout. He raised his fore-claw to catch the wrist that held the blade to his throat and twisted, forcing the weapon away. A tall narrow pine toppled as Lacerta's hips cracked against it.

'You're a fool!' Sagitta roared, his voice crackling with anger. 'This brutal plan of yours will kill everyone in the palace, just so your master can get rich!!'

'I'm sorry.'

Sagitta felt a surge of power. His frustration with Lacerta had reached its zenith and his deep-rooted knowledge connected with Lacerta's past. Sagitta began to form a sequence of events and relayed them back to Lacerta through the power of thought.

ٿٵ ٿٵ ٿٵ

He saw Dram venture out towards the coastline and watched him tackle a high mound—edged with caves and hovels which looked particularly interesting. Once inside the cavern, he was so engrossed in his discovery, that he didn't notice the tide coming in which had cut him off from the mainland. So, deciding to remain there overnight, he made a fire and cooked a couple of rabbits, but soon realised that he was not alone.

He heard the hissing first, and looking over into

the shadows, saw a huge head in the crevasse, swaying back and forth at the end of a very long neck. Dram shot up. There was nowhere for him to run to now. It was dark outside and the rising water was seeping in quickly. The creature roared and Dram fell back to the ground his hands landing in mud. The light from the fire lit up the monster and he could see that it was a hideous beast, more grotesque than anything he had seen before. The beast hissed at him and then roared, exposing the blood on her flank.

If he hadn't been so terrified, he'd have been able to appreciate her beauty more. Her colour was a deep blue, shading at the extremities and along the vanes of her wings to a deep ruby-red. But her scales looked dull and fragile, with patches of blood over them. As he looked closer he saw an egg.

'Don't touch the dragon, boy, she's protecting that egg of hers.'

Dram span round, shocked. An old man had entered the cave and came in with a fresh kill—a huge stag. The dragon reared up at the sight of the old man, her hiss of anger turning to a short bark of happiness. Hunger forced her to move closer and she lunged a bit too quickly causing the pain in her flank to bring her to an abrupt halt. But she was ravenous more than hostile, and the old man cut up the meat and threw it towards her. Injured maybe, but she was quick enough; she saw the first piece coming and snatched it right out of the air, coiling her head round to catch the second and the third.

'She was a lot worse than this when I found her,' the old man said. 'Her injuries were life-threatening with claw marks from another dragon, possibly from the mating process, possibly from an attacking female, I couldn't be sure, but I knew I had to save this incredible creature.'

'What did you do?'

'I cleaned her up, started feeding her, and now she has come to know me.'

While she was busy feeding, Dram moved to take a closer look at the egg. It rested in a corner of the cave, where only the barest top curve showed under some sand. The egg was the same colour as the sand that protected it, and the shell had a similar texture to sandstone; it was very hard, like an enormously thick bird's egg.

'Don't touch the egg,' warned the old man. 'If we go near it, she might abandon it, and we don't want that. Our role as human beings is to look after *her*.'

Dram moved away—quickly. But already a plan was germinating in his head. He knew he wasn't far from the Dragon Palace, but you could only get in there if you had a dragon. Would they take him if he had a dragon's egg?

'Why don't you take her to the Dragon Palace? I have heard it is a sanctuary now. Surely they will take care of her.'

'I can't move her, she is too sick. I have to get her better first, then we will go there and she can rear her baby in safety.'

The old man moved over to her and started to stroke her muzzle. The dragon responded and closed her eyes.

'How long have you been here?' Dram watched as the old man caressed the dragon.

'A couple of months, and I have looked after her all that time. If I leave her with anyone else, then she will die. She needs me until she has made a full recovery to look after her baby. I will not leave her.'

The female dragon snored lightly, and the old man began to stroke her head and ears, then polish the shimmering blue scales. 'I have already called her Azura, for she is the first dragon I have nurtured and she is so incredibly beautiful.' He thought his heart was going to melt. A pent up flood of emotion swept over him, and he knew he couldn't love this creature any more than if it was his own child. He had nurtured and cared for her, and now he would nurture and protect the baby when it was born. He fell asleep next to her with those wonderful thoughts weaving in his head. But Dram was not so compassionate, he had no connection with the old man or the dragon.

That's when Dram seized his opportunity. He whipped out his knife, cut the man's throat and reaching out past the slumbering giant, stuffed the valuable egg into his bag.

The mother's cries of anguish could be heard for miles.

& & &

Dram was not given the egg. He stole it in a cave. He killed a man for it. A man who was looking after your injured mother. Dram is a liar and murderer. He wants to kill you. He is going to kill you.

The black curtains that shrouded Lacerta's mind parted. He opened his eyes with a start, expecting to see Dram in front of him, preparing to kill him with an arrow dipped in tar and sulphur. His head throbbed as the events played out in his mind. 'The world is falling into a black pit of corruption, and the person who I thought had saved me, has actually destroyed me.'

Sagitta nodded his huge head. 'It would seem that way.'

'I've made a dreadful mistake. I trusted that man with my life, and I'd be foolish to think that things could go back to the way they should be. But it's the lie that hurts most of all, the idea that he raised me while keeping such an abhorrent secret. And in these moments of despair, I am already mourning the life I should have had.'

'I understand,' Sagitta said. 'And you are justified in how you are feeling.'

'Although he didn't put a knife to her throat; he didn't heed the old man's warnings. Dram killed my mother by leaving her alone.'

'He did, and I feel your pain. I too have lost my family to humans, so many of them. That is why I am here—to seek retribution and take back what is rightfully ours.'

The pain in Lacerta's head paled next to the pain in his heart. He looked at the sun high in the sky, the bright light making his head throb even more. A noise alerted him and he faced Dram— his bow flashed in the sunlight, and an arrow with crimson feathers was unbearably close.

'So now you know, and you are *all* useless to me now,' Dram cussed.

Behind him, Bard had heard everything and struggled to his feet. He launched into Dram, grappling him to the ground, but within seconds, Dram was frozen to the spot, his fighting ceased, his limbs paralysed by a force known only to him. Blood spurted from his mouth. He groaned in pain. Startled, Bard retreated quickly and watched Dram grip his stomach. A blade was protruding from his abdomen. Dram moaned a few more times, trying to speak. 'If I tell the truth now, will I find redemption in death? I know I have to take responsibility for my actions, and I'm sorry. I have always followed the wrong path in life and taken those around me down with me.' He groaned again, his voice losing strength. 'Tomorrow... Bard... the hunters... will come... at dusk. I'm so sorry...'

Bard dropped down to Dram's side. 'How many of them?'

Dram didn't answer.

'Damn you, Dram, how many hunters are there?'

Still, he didn't answer.

Bard got hold of his tunic and started to shake him. 'How many hunters are there?' Dram's eyes flew open. 'Too many for you to take on.' He tried to mouth something else but was gasping for air as his lungs slowly filled with blood.

'What is it, Dram? Tell me...'

'They want Titan, not the dragons.'

'Why?'

'Because Titan controls the silver mines all over the world. The hunters can get rich with Titan, far more than with any number of dragon scales...'

His head fell to one side—dead.

Bard fell backwards, stunned, shocked, disbelieving. All this time they had been training to protect the dragons. But did Titan know this? Did Titan have some prior knowledge from the *old ones*'? He dragged his hands down his cheeks and blew hard through his mouth. He then scrambled towards Dram, felt under his back, and retrieved the dragon's blade that Sagitta had taken from Lacerta. He looked up at the huge dragon. 'Well, you won't be needing this either.'

But Lacerta had taken the full force of the arrow. The sulphur and tar meant for Sagitta had melted his heart instantly. Sagitta roared in anger and despair and incinerated the dragon so the hunters wouldn't find him. His remains would be covered in snow. While Sagitta paid his respects and hoped Lacerta would be reunited with his mother in the afterlife, Bard cleaned the knife with the snow and put it inside his tunic belt. He then put Dram's body over Sagitta's mountainous shoulders.

'Come, Sagitta, we have to get back and tell the others.'

'What are you going to tell them?'

'That we have to protect Titan.'

CHAPTER TWENTY-ONE

Zmeitsa waded out of the river, warm water running from her golden scales. When she reached the marshy shore, she rocked back on her hind legs, opened her wings, and shook them, showering a water snake and basking frog with a monsoon of droplets. As she folded the wings neatly back to her sides, all the creatures slid back into the safety of the water. She was better now and it had not taken her as long as she'd thought it would. With the long soaks in the river, the short flights to ease her muscles back to life, and plenty of food to flesh her out, she finally felt like the Mother again. With sadness in her eyes, she looked up to the impressive Castle Dru that stood before her.

'Why are you so sad?' asked Lepus, noticing she was up and about.

'Because I won't ever see this place again.'

Lepus looked up at the monument that was home. 'But why?'

'Because none of us are coming back. It's the end of an era, and the end of the dragons of Durundal.'

'Are we all going to die?'

Zmeitsa looked at her in a melancholy way. 'In some ways, I think we are already dead.'

Lepus looked at the castle. 'Who will live here?'

'The King of Durundal will live here now. He has already been summoned by a higher force to keep the 'Seal of Kings' safe.'

'Titan?'

'Yes, like everything here, Titan decides everything.'

'What about Sirius?'

'Sirius will stay here and guard the castle like he always has done. All families need a dog don't they?'

Lepus nodded and choked back the swallow. 'When do we leave?'

'We leave tonight, Lepus, so we will have to collect as much silver as we can and store it in our sack glands.'

Lepus looked beyond the barren emptiness in front of her and saw the castle grounds spread out—as they used to be. The square outlines showed clearly in the distance, framed by fields of wheat and corn moving with the breeze. Chimney pots sent tendrils of smoke into the clear sky. A buzzard circled above, a mouse scampered below. She heard the shouts of farmworkers, the laughter of the milkmaids, and a cartload of boys were hauling another lad in as the horse pulled the wagon away. She scanned around, picturing the castle in its heyday and how willingly the youngsters had leapt at the chance to defend the castle. And then she smelled it, the burnt-out buildings and how her own family had perished in the first attack, slain for their scales; and what benefits did the scales actually provide? None whatsoever. Her mother was right. *'Where there are dragons there will be ignorance and fear, and one day the hunters will wipe them from the face of the earth forever.'*

ᘔ ᘔ ᘔ

Lepus watched Zmeitsa drop her shoulders to open her wings and then gave them a short, sharp shake to assure herself that they were working properly. She gathered herself setting her weight back and pushed off with her hind legs as she took to the sky. Lepus felt a pang of disappointment. She knew she would never see this place again. She remembered a time gone by when all the dragons would loop in wide circles over the River Dru searching for food. Their hunting was effortless and the rewards always fruitful, for the river supplied them with everything they needed—morning, noon and night. She pictured Cygnus, her crimson scales shimmering like spilt blood on a glass table, and next to her, flying in an ever-widening spiral was Lyra, her light blue skin blending into the azure sky. Lepus smiled when she remembered Delphinus, the most exquisite dragon, with a dark blue head that faded into glorious purple, which in turn faded to scarlet over her muzzle, down the underside of her jaw and covering her underbelly. Delphinus liked to soak her beautiful scales in one of the many dragon pools; some just had hot water and others had a layer of oil on the surface.

Lepus remembered those moments with affection. *Oh to soak in steaming water again, and emerge to wallow in a sandpit that peels off the old skin to leave smooth and supple scales.*

Most of the dragons enjoyed that particular luxury —for it aided growth, development and a focused mind, and Delphinus could always be found there at any time of the day.

On the shoreline, Lepus saw the image of Vega, hoisting her wings to clean underneath; her body was silver and shone like a polished sword or a highly burnished sculpture. So meticulous was her grooming routine that her blue eyes shone even brighter than her reflection. Lepus stood tall next to Vega, her golden wings spread wide to catch the sunlight. Those two would always hunt in the same spot and enjoyed that part of the riverbank where the tall rushes would scratch at their scales. Lepus smiled as she remembered them and glanced around some more, but the beauty of the scene evaporated into a disappearing veil as Zmeitsa cast a huge shadow above her.

'Come on, Lepus. They will live in our hearts forever. The hunters can't take that away from us.'

'It's hard to let go.' Lepus looked up at the Mother of Durundal, the Mother of Dragons, the great one who had nurtured all of them, the one who had shown them how to hunt and groom and take care of themselves. Zmeitsa, the oracle who knew everything, and the one everyone went to. But now it was just her; Lepus and the Mother, the youngest and the oldest, the pupil and the scholar, the learner and the wise one. But in her heart, she felt all the things that Zmeitsa had in abundance. 'I may be young, but I am not foolish, and I know that dragons will rule the world again. I can feel it.'

'You are right, Lepus. But the hare has to find the stag, and wars have to be fought and won; and only when the sorceress of the sapphire becomes the goddess of the temple, will the guiding light shine for the dragons return.'

'I don't understand, Zmeitsa.'

'It's a long way off in the future, Lepus, but your descendants will see the change.'

CHAPTER TWENTY-TWO

The Tribunes rose as Ser Alderman and his Officials strode into the council chambers, each of them carrying scrolls and documents relative to the recent events. Behind him were the Fellows, the Guardians, the Heralds, the Readers, the Temple Boys, the Master of Arms, the Steward, and the Physician. The only one missing was the Grandmaster, and it didn't go unnoticed with murmurs and assumptions brewing.

'The Grandmaster is not feeling well, and has asked to be excused as we discuss the torrid matter in hand.' Ser Alderman was keen to settle the tense atmosphere that was building, the questions about the Grandmaster's ill health palpable.

As soon as everyone was assembled, Ser Alderman nodded his head for those who could to sit down, and the rest to stand while he conducted the proceedings. No sooner had the Guardians and Temple Boys arranged themselves behind the Officials than the Master of Arms, rose abruptly.

'Ser Alderman, have you established when the attack will be?'

Ser Alderman pushed himself to his full height. 'Tomorrow at dusk.'

'Then we do not have much time.'

'No, we do not.'

'What are we going to do?' The Steward shouted as he rose to his feet, his eyes flaring wide. 'Gentlemen, please, if I may.'

The Steward slumped back in his chair and locked eyes with the Master of Arms.

Ser Alderman waited for silence. 'Thank you.' He scanned the table and found Bard. 'Please, Bard tell everyone exactly what happened.

Bard rose and bowed to Ser Alderman. 'Officials, Tribunes, Ser Alderman. Yesterday I was part of a mission to discover the whereabouts of the hunters. I was assigned to go with Dram and Lacerta. Everything was going well. I had no reason to suspect that anything was wrong and both Dram and Lacerta seemed calm and relaxed about the mission. Lacerta seemed feisty at first, but I put that down to his exhilaration to get going. Though as we were nearing Storma Bay, I started to think that Lacerta was ramming Sagitta. I tried to contact the control tower but the signal was blocked. I couldn't get through. Then Dram shot me with a dart that knocked me unconscious. Sagitta took me directly to the ground, but that was all part of Dram's master plan.'

Shocked faces spun around, disbelieving of what they had heard.

Bard continued. 'I came to, only to find Dram with an arrow pointed at the dragons, they had been discussing something between themselves, but I had to stop Dram from committing this crime so I grappled him to the ground. He fell on a dagger intended to kill Sagitta. In his final moments, he told me that the hunters were gathering to attack us tomorrow at dusk. When I asked him how many, he said there would be too many for us to take on.'

More shocked faces rotated from side to side. Ser Alderman held up his hand for silence. 'But that's not all.' Bard looked at the pitiful faces of those that had become his friends, his confidants, his mentors, his family; and tried desperately to compose himself. He took a deep breath and found his voice. 'They are coming for Titan. They don't want the dragons, it's all been a ruse to get us out into the open and away from the observation tower.'

'So they can sweep in?' The master-of-arms sank back in his chair, everything about him suddenly looking hollow.

'Exactly.' Bard sat down and felt the heavy weight of despair on his own breaking shoulders.

The room became a tomb of silence. The scrolls sprang back into their neat little rolls and the documents floated across the table on a breeze. Worthless information that would be better served on a raging fire.

'What shall we do?'

Ser Alderman stood up. 'We are *all* needed now. It's not just the dragons and those that can ride them. It's every man for himself, for the man beside him, in front of him, and behind him. Titan has chosen every one of us, we must remember that. Titan has summoned us all for this one special day. Titan knew this was going to happen and made men out of us so we could stand up and protect it. We know that every man here is trained in the art of warfare; so every man must take up his chosen weapon and defend with it. We cannot let these hunters win. We cannot be overthrown. I would rather watch the complex disappear into the ground than see the hunters take ownership.

They might be an army of many men. They might have weapons and armour and a force of evil running through their veins, but we have all been trained by masters of their craft. We have discipline, we have knowledge, we are a united family under the watchful eye of our Grandmaster; and those qualities will go a long way over the next twenty-four hours—but most importantly, they *will* help us protect Titan.'

CHAPTER TWENTY-THREE

The sun hung low and red in the sky when Lepus woke. From her resting place on the hill she could see the Dragon Palace casting a long sinister shadow across the land. Zmeitsa was reclining against a tree, though she was so perfectly camouflaged with her golden skin and tawny scales that she blended in against the tree trunk.

'How long did I nap?' Lepus asked.

'Not long,' Zmeitsa replied. 'Only a couple of hours.'

'I only meant to rest my eyes for a moment.'

'I don't begrudge you the sleep, I know how hard it is to keep going with bags of silver to carry.'

'Are we where we need to be?'

'Yes, we are where we need to be, but we have to go down to the shoreline first.'

There was an unnatural mist here, which didn't feel right to either of them.

'I do not like this at all,' said Lepus.

'It will be all right,' said Zmeitsa. 'Stay close to me.'

'I can taste the despair here, the death, the sadness, the decay, the cold. There are restless spirits in the air and tormented souls below the water.'

Zmeitsa slowed her wings. 'The cursed hate the warm and seek more dammed souls to join them.'

'Was that meant to make me feel better?'

'No, just saying what sort of place this is. So follow me as I find what I am looking for.'

The shore was all sharp rocks and glowering cliffs, and the Dragon Palace stood on the very top of the highest point; its towers, walls, and bridges quarried from a white alabaster stone that was a rare find in the thousand-year-old caves. One thousand steps ascended from the shore while the angry waves foamed and crashed below them. Not for the faint-hearted, these steps served to keep the young men fit, and the hunters out. The shoreline was a mass of jagged nooks and crannies which together with the crashing waves, tried their damnedest to block Zmeitsa's path as she sought out the deepest cavern. Soon, inside a deep dark hollow, where the air was cold and damp, there was a strong smell of death and an even stronger one of decay.

'It's very cold in here,' said Lepus. 'It's giving me the creeps.'

'Windy cold and damp. A miserable place and exactly what I am looking for.'

'Zmeitsa, look!'

'What? Show me.'

Lepus pointed to the remains of a female dragon with a human skeleton at her side; and a newer, fresher skeleton of a baby dragon was curled up beside her.

'Is that what you are looking for?'

'This poor dragon died in pain and agony, and I can only imagine her suffering, but I know there is someone close by who can help us. We need to go down a lot further.'

They were making their way to the great stone city of Hydra, with its monoliths and sepulchres which had sunk beneath the waves, and the deep waters full of colossal statues and great caverns, all of which had been hidden from the outside world for millennia. It was here that Hydra lived on the other side of an immense carved door with a she-dragon bas-relief, ornate lintel, patterned threshold, and the skulls of a thousand men around it.

As many times as Zmeitsa had heard about it, she had always wanted to see it. The chambers in the cave were large, airy, and littered with the bounty from reefed ships and the misery that went with it. Two serpents stood like guards, carrying silver tridents instead of spears; though what they could do to protect one as powerful as Hydra was a source of amusement for Zmeitsa. Lepus had to stay with the guards while another guard took Zmeitsa past faded banners, broken shields, rusted swords of old, and hundreds of wooden figureheads that once adorned the prows of ships. Two golden mermaids flanked Hydra's court, and as the guards created a portal in the sea mist, a herald announced her name.

'Zmeitsa—Mother of Durundal, Mother of Dragons.'

As Zmeitsa entered Hydra's court she couldn't help but notice everything nautical around her. The cave walls were adorned with an assortment of broken helms, starfish, shellfish and other crustaceans. She felt bones crushing beneath her feet as she waded through the stagnant water, seaweed stuck to her talons, and she accidentally kicked away skulls with sea snakes burrowing into the sockets. A range of enormous megalodon jaws hung from the ceiling, each one of the two hundred and fifty teeth supporting a twelve-inch flickering flame.

The dais was a battered old war galley, with broken steps up to the throne, the ragged sails hung like royal drapes and dim lanterns were positioned around the slimy taffrails. The throne was made from the skeletons of whales and cushioned with the carcasses of at least a dozen octopods; Hydra sat there in her splendour displaying her new toxic silver-grey scales. One of her heads was feasting on entrails, one exposing gore and slime on the fangs and the other four were weaving their way closer to the dragon who was now dwarfed by her incredible size. Her neck rose, one of the fanged mouths opened, and a stench of rot and decay accompanied a woman's voice.

'Zmeitsa, you are most welcome to my humble abode.'

'Thank you, Hydra, for allowing me to enter your domain, it is most gracious of you.'

Hydra grabbed a giant squid from a tank of water and offered it to Zmeitsa. 'Please, you must be hungry after your long journey.'

The dragon caught it with her huge jaw and swallowed it whole.

'So what can I do for you, Zmeitsa?'

Zmeitsa breathed out a plume of smoke which cast a temporary heat over the chilly surroundings.

'Hydra, I need your help.'

'What for? How can I help the great Zmeitsa?'

'We go back a long way, Hydra.'

Hydra reached round for another squid, the tentacles desperately clinging onto the life-saving tank. But it was futile. 'I know… that's why I saved your sons when they attacked me.'

'They were trying to save the dragon, they weren't attacking you.'

'Hmmm…' Hydra remembered hearing Bard telling Ijja to leave *her* alone, that they were on *her* territory.'

'It was that foolish boy I was after. I had seen him before; horrible, nasty, no empathy, no soul.'

Zmeitsa caught the look of pity in a fragile existence, one that Hydra had not intended for herself.

'You have just described yourself, Hydra.'

The six heads shot forward and circled the dragon's head, the teeth snapping furiously and a foul stench coming from somewhere within. 'It's taken me months to recover from the attack—months. I have stayed down here waiting for my limbs to grow again. Hideous as it may sound, they do grow again, and bigger and more monstrous than before. I wish I could die and end this suffering that curses me every single day. But it will never happen, and I have to accept that I will stay in this form forever.'

'I know, Hydra, I understand. I too have endured months of convalescing after an attack on my home. But unlike you, I grow weaker with each attack, and so do the dragons.'

Both females retreated, considering their plight.

After the longest pause, the dragon spoke. 'There will be hunters descending on the Dragon Palace very soon. They want to take Titan. These hunters have no heart, no soul, no empathy, just like the young man you killed. But the dragons do not have the ability to disable these men. They do not have the numbers either. But with your help, they can rid the kingdoms of these parasites.

'I do not want to do that anymore. I do not want to get involved with matters that do not concern me. I do not want to grow even more monstrous with every attack I am subjected to.'

'But what if they bring more, and try to find you? If they control Titan, then they can rule you!'

Hydra laughed out loud, all six heads spiralled to the ceiling, and the hideous chandeliers with their darts of flame shook above her cackle as her legs and torso rose from her throne in the exertion.

She circled the dragon. 'I would like to see them try,' came the chilling response.

'If you do this for me, then I can take the curse away.'

Hydra stopped circling. She froze within inches of Zmeitsa.

One head with one tearful eye looked straight at the dragon. 'You can make me human again?'

'Yes.'

'You promise me?'

'Of course I do.'

'Because you know what will happen if you deceive me.'

She rose higher and the rest of her body slithered off the deck, the six heads sniffing around the enclosure, her twelve legs following her monstrous bulbous frame through the cavern.

'What are you doing, Hydra?'

'I am making room for you and your two sons if I find out that you are lying to me.'

The dragon roared and shook the enclosure. Hydra shrank back to the safety of her throne.

'I do not lie, Hydra, I do not need to lie. We are friends that go back a long way. I respect you. I love you. I would *never* lie to you. We are both females in a monster's body, and I give you my word, if you help me… then I will help you.'

'Even as a beast you are beautiful, Zmeitsa.' Hydra willed her voice to carry on despite the sadness. 'I was beautiful once.'

'I know you were, and I know that beneath that tough outer shell you still are.'

'I'm not, Zmeitsa, look at me. I'm a black, shiny, monstrous shape that slithers and crawls like a misshapen serpent straight out of the pits of hell.'

'But doing something good will bring out that inner beauty. It will change you.'

'How can it?' Hydra sank back on her throne. 'I am consumed with anger, hatred, and everything evil. My heart aches when memories surface. I have nothing to be thankful for.'

'Then change.'

Hydra leaned forward. 'I am not you, Zmeitsa. Everything about you is good and beautiful and radiant. Every single one of your scales is a tiny work of art, your eyes see hope, your heart is pure, your memories are good, your family love you. I, I have nothing.'

Zmeitsa moved forward and ignored the crossed spears forbidding her entrance onto the royal dais.

Hydra didn't even notice with all of her heads down-cast, her black hearts consumed with hatred, and if she'd been able to swallow the mighty ocean and send it to the dark mass in the sky above then she would do it in an instant. This was her home now, many fathoms beneath the surface of the sea—and she hated it.

Zmeitsa leaned closer to Hydra and breathed a veil of thick silvery mist over her. It slid over her skin as if caressing her and instantly she began to shine; a glimmer of a smile broke through her cavernous mouths, and her bulbous eyes saw love for the first time. Her arms wanted to reach out and embrace it all, to encapsulate it and hold onto it forever. The brume made a crackling sound as it settled on the royal dais and a wave of silver turned the skulls and bones and discarded entrails into intricate treasures of exquisite beauty. But as Hydra reached out for them and marvelled at her new surroundings, they started to evaporate and gradually melted away.

'There is hope for you, Hydra, and I can help you. But only if you help me first.'

CHAPTER TWENTY-FOUR

It was a cool day in the Dragon Palace in Bergen. In the distance, south of the palace, the foothills below the mountain range were crowned with slow-moving clouds, grey against the whites and yellows of the coastal mountains. Ethereal bands of rain hung like veils from the sky. In a light airy chamber, the Grand-master watched the rain drift steadily eastwards, and away from the grand apartments.

From her room, she could hear the orchestra, and the beautiful harmonies of the choir filtered through the walls. She lifted the veil high above her head and looked in the mirror. A beautiful face was etched with sadness for there was nothing more that she could do. This time, she would have to trust Titan. The bewitching dress of ivory silk clung to her body like a whisper and accentuated her shape like a second skin. And for all the dazzling jewels that radiated extravagance, for every stitch and button, crease and fold, created with chafed fingers and milky eyes ruined from working by candlelight—a woman hidden from the world looked back. Today, she would go to her private chapel and ask for guidance in these troubled times. She went to the window, and throwing it wide open she breathed in the cool mountain air. She wanted to see another day here, another year, another lifetime; for if she didn't then she would surely die. But today—dying was not an option.

She stroked her dagger with a finger, it was razor sharp and wickedly cruel. A smile tugged at her lips and she kissed the murderous blade. Her companion had been found in the walls of the temple many years ago and would serve her well today. She stroked it one last time and tucked it up her sleeve. Then she faced the door and waited to be escorted to her bathing room. On exactly the stroke of five, the eunuchs arrived. And as per usual, they fixed the veil on her head, cloaked her body, and covered her hands, so to anyone who saw her she was a beast in human clothing.

On the way, she stopped a while to listen to the

exquisite harpist and lingered in awe at the sonorous sounds of the cellist. Two young maidens scattered petals at her feet as she made her way through the passageway. A soprano held a high octave as she continued her journey.

Statues in fountains were placed inside the Grandmaster's bathing room, and the fragrance of aromatic petals and essential oils wafted around the enclosure. A deep, pristine white, enamel tub, stood on four enormous claw feet. Two ornate gold taps in the shape of fire breathing dragons bubbled in the corner as it was being filled. The Grandmaster looked out of the window, and from her high elevation, stretching out before her, lay the magnificent grounds of the palace.

The glow from the sun had dappled the grass a sheen of silver, and the jewelled spire of the citadel shone like a beacon reaching up to the sky. She remembered how laughter had once echoed through the corridors. While outside, the ghosts of a thousand onlookers admired her from afar for fear of discovering her terrible secret. She watched for a while before casting an eye around the beautiful room. The carved marble walls still mesmerised her with their golden inlays of dragons, wild beasts and mythical figures. The domed ceiling reached up to the rafters and resembled a twilight evening with myriad stars and constellations and she smiled as she remembered the most recent dragons named after a particular constellation: Pavo—the peacock; what a proud boy he was, and Noctua—the moth, the beautiful female. Lacerta—the lizard, how well Dram had ridden him, and Lupus—the wolf, what a tornado he had been in his youth. Antares—the stag; Sli had been good to handle him. Pardalis, the leopard, camouflaged himself on so many occasions. Then there was Mensa, the table mountain, the biggest and most formidable of all the dragons she had ever known; she sighed at the presence she commanded. Pyxis the compass, could find her way anywhere. The enchanting Bellatrix—a female warrior; what a fighter she had been, and then Sagitta, the arrow, and he had stolen Bella's heart as well. She sighed at the memory and went back to the bath and, as she always did, tested the water with her hand. As she shrugged out of her robe it pooled on the polished marble floor in a whisper. Stepping into the water, the pungent oils separated and the petals rushed to her skin. Sinking down, she let the water flow over her body and breathed in the sweetest aroma of cinnamon, rose water, honey and hyacinth. She closed her eyes and leant her head back against the roll of the lip. A sigh eased out of her throat, and the warmth settled into her thoughts and body, melting away all the stresses of the past few days. She thought of the ancestors before her and wiped away the tears. *I'm so sorry that I could not protect what you fought so hard to keep. I am sorry that this palace, this rock, this home of homes is now to crumble at the hands of the hunters, those who do not know the meaning of life and empathy.* She closed her eyes and held the ancestors there. *Could we have done anything differently, or does everything come to an end, everything except the constellations in the sky?* She reached out for an answer, the voices just a breath away. The drips from her fingers rippled into the bathwater, creating swirls among the delicate frangipani petals and dispersing as quickly as they had come. *Nothing lasts forever, nothing at all.*

Two eunuchs came in with plump clean towels, jewels, and accessories, while another carried her gown over two outstretched arms. They busied themselves arranging the attire while the Grandmaster dried herself in front of a full-length gilt-edge mirror. Leading her into the dressing area, a chair was provided in front of a long marble table. Here lay an assortment of combs and brushes, powders and perfume bottles. And as her hand lightly touched the exquisite array of jewels, she sat down as she had done a hundred times before, while her long fair hair was brushed and curled so it fell down her back in soft ringlets. Pearls were clipped to her earlobes, a blue diamond necklace was secured around her small neck, and a jadeite ring slipped onto her finger. And as she eased into her purple gown and slippers, she heard the siren wail to warn of the impending attack.

CHAPTER TWENTY-FIVE

In an instant, the brutal impact of the warning siren took precedence. Mensa sprang quickly. Lupus was instantly behind her. Then all the dragon's were in the air and Titan groaned as it watched the formation tighten up to guard it.

'Protect Titan,' rang out Ser Alderman's orders. Remember that our ancestors were a lot smarter than we are, we must protect it.'

The Dragon Palace began to shake, in small tremors at first, but then more noticeably. 'It's only Titan activating the electromagnetic field,' assured a Fellow. 'All is well.'

Sagitta clocked eyes with Bard. 'I have to get Bella-trix and Pyxis,' he said. 'With the masonry this unstable they might get trapped in the infirmary.'

'Yes, you must go and get them. I will be okay.'

'I'll be as quick as I can.'

The palace was shaking occasionally and the earth rumbled in many parts. Sagitta flew into the main enclosure and followed the path to the infirmary. The door was blocked from the inside.

'Bella, are you in there?'

'Sagitta… thank goodness you are here. Something dreadful has happened. Bella is hurt, the Physician is dead, and I am not strong enough to open the door.'

'Stand clear, Pyxis. I will blast it open.'

'I can't move, Sagitta, I am hurt as well.'

'I will have to push it then.'

The door moved under the pressure of his heavy shoulder, and as he pushed his way in, bars of light pierced the fractured mortar and made motes of dust glitter where they hung in the air. Scorch marks plastered the walls, the floor and the ceilings, and pockets of soot stood in piles where crumpled documents had been torched. The paintings, masterworks and tapestries had been ripped from their hooks and desecrated, while the tomes and other ancient volumes lay in shreds under the huge mahogany bookcases. The Physician sat at his table, his face in a pool of blood, his hand on a lethal concoction of chemicals and dynamite. A ticking clock was attached.

'The Physician went mad; he locked us in, then started shouting and screaming about blowing this place up. We appealed to him to stop but he wouldn't listen. Bella went to prevent him from preparing the deadly concoction, but he slashed at her before he turned the knife on himself. I tried to help her but the building was falling around me.'

Sagitta heard another rumble and when he saw Bella's bloodied body he roared, a roar that would not stop. Fire and smoke came from his throat, and he thrashed about and tore down everything in his path as he raced to make his way to her. His heart pounded furiously, trying to beat its way out of his chest, and with every roar, a new flame shot from his mouth. Helplessly, he moved ever closer, his breaking heart full of agony and hatred, every roar reverberating through the room. His eyes fell on his love. Seeing her slashed and torn body where it had only just healed was too much for him, and the cry that came from him dwarfed every sound he had made before. He looked closer—she didn't seem to be breathing—and it took every bit of strength to pull her up into his arms. He lifted her. 'Bella, Bella, can you hear me?'

Nothing came back.

'We have to get her out of here, Pyxis, follow me.'

Pyxis tried to lift her head. 'Sagitta, look at me. I will not survive. Take Bella—and quickly.'

Sagitta hadn't even noticed the heavy pole that had gone right through her chest. He struggled with the decision, his mind was racing and panicking. 'I will come back for you, Pyxis, I promise.'

'There is no time… save yourselves… take Bella to safety… this place will blow any minute.'

Sagitta looked back at the Physician and now knew what the ticking clock meant. 'If I go now then I will have time.'

🐾 🐾 🐾

Turbulence, savage, ruthless, destructive; a pressure inexorable and deadly. A churning mass of armour clunked and rattled as it got closer, bearing torches that advanced like an endless ring of fire. Fear! Terror! A primeval longing! A scream was torn from a single throat, a scream like a knife severing every nerve individually. The invisible assailant then sliced into more throats as he took them down from behind.

'Help me!' A pitiful cry came from cords lacerated by an extreme force. One brave soul went to the Guardian's rescue. He didn't make it and gurgled his last breath as the Guardian reached out to him.

Higher up, Pavo could not see. His eyes were filled with blood from vessels burst by the force of his cry to alert another victim. He had seen the arrow coming, gathering velocity with every insidious length; a shot as fatal as the ones before.

Bard was on the ground and turned to see a huge spear flashing through the air as fast and straight as a ray of light. It dug into his side, sending him to his knees. He gave a pained cry as he grabbed the spear with both hands, struggling with its weight. He tried to summon Sagitta but he knew that he would be with Bella and Pyxis ushering them to safety. His energy waned as he felt the fire raging inside him, his body was getting colder... then he passed out.

Half blinded as he was, Pavo dropped to the ground and Davio ran over to Bard's bleeding body. His flesh was cold and clammy to the touch.

'He isn't breathing,' Davio cried. 'His lips are blue!'

'*He's alive though*!' came Pavo's thought. '*I know that he is still alive.*'

Some half-forgotten memory prompted Davio to roll Bard on his back and open his mouth. He then covered his mouth with his own and exhaled into his throat. He saw Bard's chest rise and fall with each exhale. The dragon could feel Davio's anguish. He watched as Davio breathed in and out, conscious of the procedure and taking his time, even with everything going on around him; the noise, the clamour, the yelling, the shouting.

'Davio! He's breathing for himself now, Davio! Pavo's cry was cut short as he took an arrow to the chest. Davio spun around and took a fatal shaft through his neck. Pavo was still alive and roared at his attackers. They came at him again, ramming their spears into his heavy scaling. He staggered around them, whipping his neck from side to side, sending one man flying to his death and flattening another; all the while his tail was sweeping and his head was roaring, but he knew his strength was waning and against so many, they could easily overpower him now. He roared again, but it only alerted more hunters and they set their spears to kill and ran towards him.

The hunters were advancing with ceaseless violence. Their weapons of deadly poison found the weak spots on the dragons. Titan began to vibrate, a force underground began to send tremors through the soil, and as the electromagnetic field charged up its energy, those in armour were quickly sucked into the earth. Weapons of steel were plucked from the air and disappeared with them. Dragons were rising in unison, destroying many with flaming breath.

Still, the invading army advanced. Despite the

metal being sucked into the depths of the earth core by Titan's magnetic field, there were still huge numbers advancing.

By now the Officials were retreating. Bard was alone on the ground with no one to defend him. A hunter was close to Bard and held a long, curved knife in one hand, a whip in another. The whip was whirled in a half circle and raced around Bard's neck before anyone knew what had happened. With a savage yank, the hunter jerked Bard forwards and placed a huge boot on his throat, pinning him to the ground.

Out yonder, ascending from the outer edge of the cliff, the Mother rose with anger in her eyes and flames of fire pouring from her throat. The hunter was incinerated instantly as the Mother flattened him under her talons and landed in a protective stance over her son, kicking out with her powerful back legs. The glands of silver were like acid to the hunters and the spray devoured many on the spot. Lepus flew above her and sprayed the injured dragons—the effect was swift and accurate. The membranes knotted together and the scales were replaced quickly—still the army advanced. The structure began to tremble again, and more chunks of masonry began to fall. Ser Alderman looked at the ever-increasing army swarming like cannibal ants.

At the same time, Zmeitsa became aware of more men moving up on her; they were trying to surround her. One ran forward, a spear in his hands, but she had Bard beneath her so dare not rear up and leave him vulnerable. Instead, she threw back her great head and snapped it forward to release a cloud of venom. It went a long way but some of the hunters got through and surged at her in a wild charge. With her son beneath her, she could only spin around tightly in the same spot. She would not leave him exposed. As her tail lashed out on the counterattack, the hunters continued to pierce her skin with their wooden spears tipped with tar and sulphur. At that moment, all she could sense from them was an incarnate right to kill, fuelled with fear and bloodlust. Fear is responsible for all ignorance and hatred, she thought and swept her tail hard, but more hunters gathered in the attack. Mensa became aware of the relentless bombardment and hovered over Zmeitsa in a defensive role as Ramou fired weapon after weapon.

Alto was battling with a hunter and choked as a knife sank squarely into his shoulder, paralysing him instantly. He pulled the knife free and staggered backwards, and then Noctua came in and slammed into the perpetrator. Alto sank the knife to the hilt into the assailant's body.

'Take this!' he shouted, pulling the knife free and driving it home again.

'And this!' The knife once more plunged into the hunter's gut.

'And this!'

'And this!'

The hunter gurgled and spat out blood. 'This is just the beginning. If you look out yonder, there are even more storming in, to take your Titan and the Dragon Palace.' The hunter's voice seemed to fade, washed away by the roar from Alto. But as Alto stood up, his feet awash with blood and urine he saw them—a monstrous battalion advancing.

As the recruits advanced, Saul shouted out the order to Sli and Dom. They were on the target range and had spent all night setting up an ambush. On his command, they cut the heavy rope holding the long line of batons down and on release a deadly spiked trap flew in the air and stopped the hunters in their tracks.

The men screamed in terror. Many shouted to retreat, but as they did so Sli and Dom ran alongside them to unleash a second trap. The caged hunters spun round desperately, but every route of escape was blocked by the impassable rows of murderous batons. Many of the hunters stumbled and fell and were trampled to death, some had already become impaled on the spikes. The Tribunes did what damage they could with the weapons they had, and the dragons flew in to torch the line of immobilised men.

Sagitta staggered out with Bellatrix in his arms. He saw Bard beneath the Mother, looked at Bella, and remembering her dream, he knew that Bard was still alive. At that moment, Bella felt the silver particles falling in the air and subconsciously she breathed them in, and mixing with the blood of Sagitta, her injuries began to heal. Lepus saw Sagitta and flew over, administering more of the life-saving droplets.

'We don't have much time, Sagitta, your friend must come with me, I can keep her safe.' Sagitta trusted Lepus with his life, and if she said she could keep Bella safe, then she would.

'It's not far, just below us in a cave.'

'I have to go back for her sister.'

Just then, behind him, there was a great roar as the air turned into an inferno. The blast that came from the infirmary would have seared and blinded any eye that glimpsed it. Stone turned to vapour instantly, and the earth quivered like a living thing. The groaning ground rose, thrusting the burning lava ever upward. The rapid chemical combustion of dynamite and chemicals caused molten rock to spew into the air, shrieking and howling as if to turn the sky into granite. Where the infirmary had once stood, there was nothing except a crater in the ground and molten lava still gushing from its core.

Before Lepus had finished speaking, the second wave of hunters spewed over the target range in their hordes.

'Follow Lepus. She can take you to safety. I can't have you dying on me as well.' He watched them disappear from view, then braced himself with the others and roared out his flames, but it was useless against so many. The hunters aimed their weapons and fired. The survivors could only watch in terror. The monoliths began to crumble. A sign of defeat —surely.

A flaming arrow was curled into the night sky, and a shivering hiss of blades leaving their scabbards responded to its cue. Hell was unleashed. Arrows curved down from the hillside, sending fireballs of oil-soaked liniment into the palace, the impact brutal as an orange ball of flame exploded across the courtyard scattering the splintered frames of ancient enclosures.

The palace was ablaze and continued to burn as more arrows were fired. Like streams of lava from an erupting volcano, the army descended. Arrows flew their course and plunged into the chaos of shrieking people and stricken dragons. Many were trying to control the fire, and others screamed in agony as they became engulfed in flames. Brave men ran in to thwart the siege, but unforgiving swords hacked into the beaten Officials. Silver blades and gold-tipped daggers sliced through muscle, and a thousand booted feet stampeded the life out of prostrate wounded bodies.

Amongst the slaughter, a waft of black smoke rose in the air and wove its way through the empty corridors, suffocating everything in its path.

In the royal apartments, the Grandmaster froze as the eunuchs tried to calm her.

She shook her head in despair. 'I don't think our forces can cope with this. You must go to the hills and save yourselves.'

But the eunuchs shook their heads, they weren't going anywhere.

Time was running out, the sound of death was fast approaching, and now there were no more options. She donned the veil and cloak, slipped the dagger inside her glove, and made for her private chapel to pray. The terrifying sounds of slaughter compelled her to run faster. People were spinning in all directions, dodging fire tipped arrows and falling debris. She summoned her servants to run faster. Frantic and confused they ran into a wall of arrows and dropped down dead.

The air was claustrophobic with smoke, and shallow pools of debris littered the way like old, abandoned toys. The Grandmaster picked her way through them as carefully as she could, avoiding the six-foot-long nails that protruded like hideous flags of honour, and blocks of black basalt so large that they must have taken twenty dragons to hoist them into place. The main tower collapsed behind her, and as she ran through the broken masonry, she yelled out for Ser Alderman. But no one could hear her cries. No one at all.

Outside, there still raged screams and cries, running footsteps, the sounds of death and the dying. She was now at the concealed entrance. The door was heavy and already had piles of asphalt blocking its access. She had to open it to speak with her loved ones. She dropped to her knees and pawed at the fallen masonry with her bare hands.

She crawled in amongst the dust and debris, and pushing herself to her full height, closed the door firmly behind her. She turned around, pressed her back against the door and closed her eyes. Now it was silent. Not one sound could filter in from the hell outside. Just as the 'great ones' had kept the Dragon

Palace warm and harmonious, they also kept this place silent and cool. She stayed there for a while and tried to calm her frantic heart. Her breathing returned to normal and she took a huge breath of air. Feeling safe at last, she opened her eyes and gazed in wonder at the beautiful silver carvings on the walls; a hare, a wolf, a leopard, a stag, and an exquisite mosaic of a moth; each one decorated and embellished with rare stones and priceless jewels. On the other side were more carvings with elaborate details and embellishments; a maiden, a mother, a crone, a goddess, and a beautiful depiction of rebirth. At every corner and every niche, the sculpture of a dragon stood proud; made out of onyx, jade and amber, she stopped a while to marvel at the workmanship and lingered in awe at the beautiful creations that the 'great ones' had crafted all those centuries ago. She touched each one to make that connection and seek the answers that her soul demanded. The power from the stone radiated around her body and a smile tugged at her lips.

The entrance fed into a long chamber lit by lamps fixed along the walls, each one flickering into life as it detected her presence. A smell of sweetness cloyed the air, and a tense silence amplified her footsteps as they brushed against the uneven flagstones. The aisle led to a throne, and she fanned out her cloak behind her and took to her seat. Now, she could view her domain from another angle, and that's when she heard the ethereal voice.

'Do not fear, oh great one, I am but a breath away. The beast will be reborn.'

CHAPTER TWENTY-SIX

Water dripped in the distance, hollow splashes echoing and re-echoing, and a creature rose from the murk, a creature so hideous that there didn't seem to be an end to the body. The smell of decay followed, and anyone in proximity would not have been able to breathe for the stench was unlike anything they had experienced before and it clung to skin like oil. Overhead, the chemical clouds had turned streaky black, gritty heat was burning skin, and the dust from the blast still rose in mini tornados and clogged the throats of men.

The invading army was gathering momentum, and with a promise to keep, a huge dark figure loomed over the ever-increasing battleground. Six heads appeared first, the sharp rows of teeth bared in loud rumbling snarls, others were chattering and grinding together. The eyes, kindled with a killing light were bulbous and searching for blood. Long snaky necks rose higher and higher, weaving and winding as droplets of seawater fell from the twelve blubbery arms. As the body emerged further from the sea, its endless torso was supported on a huge tail with a single talon at the end. Standing at over fifteen metres tall with a range that quadrupled that, she threw back her heads, staring into the twilight sky above, and slowly, electric energy began to gather and accumulate around her. She called on all her strength and forced her mind far and wide, sucking the power from the electromagnetic field. The sky seemed to thicken and roil like an enormous body of water, and then the energy started to fall from the sky, crackling and snapping as it tumbled towards the ogre below. It hit her with an alarming force, shaking and vibrating as the ions spread throughout her body. The twelve electrically charged arms opened wide, quivering, trembling, holding onto the power within. Then, with an almighty surge, the lightning erupted and struck the army before her, blasting them aside, burning and scorching, blackening skin and igniting cloth, hair and weapons.

Turning slowly as the surges continued, Hydra

directed the scything force to carve a path through the battlefield and stormed into the chaos ripping the advancing army to pieces. The heads lurched forward and ripped out throats, the twelve hands shredded skin on contact. The rotating arms snapped bodies in two. Lengths of steel were thrust through ribs, shafts of wood caved in skulls. She felt a throat crushing beneath her talon and tasted the blood when it spurted upwards. Then she reached for a length of rope that was secured to her side; in an instant, all twelve arms were rotating and rounding up scores of men who were decapitated first then catapulted into the sea. Her reign of terror was still not done and taking a handful of wicked blades from another pouch at her massive girth, each one severed a main artery on contact. A hunter screamed, a wordless scream that was not of this world, and without thinking, leapt at Hydra. All rational thought was gone and the axe was like a feather in her hand. As he was thrown to the sea with his head caved in, his weapon was sent on a collision course that did not end until another twenty men had met their deaths. A second bubbling scream marked a hunter who had come in too close, followed by a third, a fourth, and a fifth; their final moments played out as headless bodies stumbling around before toppling over into their graves. With the monster obliterating the army in seconds, the surviving dragons, Tribunes and Officials, launched into the attack. Lepus followed with more sacks of silver, which on contact with the hunters devoured their ranks but healed the dragons.

The dragons' jaws closed on the throats of the hunters who were now blinded by the chemical reaction and their skin burning from the silver vapour.

In less than an hour, it was over. The army had been swiftly taken care of. All the hunters were eradicated, though it wasn't without their own casualties, and the surviving eunuchs had to go round and collect their dead. Hydra disappeared back into the sea to tend to her burnt and disfigured body, and wash the blood from her mouths and claws, for the hour was approaching to be transformed into human form again, and she needed to look her best.

CHAPTER TWENTY-SEVEN

The night was now clear, the clouds blown aside. Above them, the moon continued her journey and the stars lit the way for her. Life and death merged at this spot, a tangle of unresolved endings and unfinished lives. The smell of death hung in the air but rebirth wasn't far away.

The dragons assembled at the perimeter of the burning ground. This ceremonial field was a circle many hundreds of yards across, the ground now permanently blackened with the soot of many generations of funeral pyres. The surviving Officials, Tribunes and eunuchs stood around the edges, their robes and faces smeared with blood, sweat and tears. At the centre of the dark circle was a tower of pine logs and on the top, those who had perished.

'Light the pyre,' Ser Alderman said.

'What about the Grandmaster?'

Ser Alderman shook his head.

One of each of the Officials put their torches to the kindling. The fire ate hungrily, rising quickly up the stacked wood to lick at the limbs, hair, and blood of the fallen. Ser Alderman opened the ancient leather-bound book he held. He spoke the words without ever glancing down at the text. 'Fire is a life-giving energy, a force to create new life. It protects us with its light when we are afraid, it comforts us with its warmth when we are cold, it cooks our food to provide energy when we are hungry. But it also has the power to take life away. We have witnessed today how many will use evil as a way of gaining power. We have watched them destroy our home, our legacy, our roots—with hatred. Those same people who took the lives of our bravest warriors: the Officials, the eunuchs, Tribune Davio, plus our dragons: Pavo, Pyxis and Lacerta. Let us not forget Haynes who lost his life at sea, as well as Ijja and Dram who chose another path, but are already on the other side. Now, as is our custom, we ask that these flames of fire take these brave souls to their final resting place, to sit with their ancestors, and guide us as we follow a new path. Where this path will take us we do not know, but with the flame of light, warmth and energy, we will continue until we are reunited in the afterlife.' He paused while everyone watched the sparks rising from the pyre to mix among the stars. 'Take your time to say your goodbyes, dear friends, I know that the Grandmaster will want to speak with you soon.'

He spoke quietly with the survivors and circulated slowly as he embraced with the mourners. Tears of sadness and despair were heavy, but the will to live was strong. With so much death, the importance of winning the war was hard to convey, and Ser Alderman knew that now, more than at any other time, the people needed their Grandmaster. He looked past the staggering survivors, broken, wounded, stained with blood and dirt, and then he saw a building bathed in light and knew where the Grandmaster was.

⁂

A cathedral-like hall away from the main palace, it was one of the last buildings standing in its entirety. He pushed the door open and glanced down the aisle. The Grandmaster's throne was a giant, gilded pedestal, draped with blood-red satin. Her body was slumped on the seat, her head lowered to the floor, eyes fixed on the doorway in which Ser Alderman stood. Her expression was blank as if she were numb with shock, her purple cape draped to each side, spreading onto the floor like a carpet. Her hands clutched her breast as if she were feeling her breaking heart and the flickering light gave the illusion that she had feathery scales ruffling in a breeze. At her side was a dagger, short, deadly and quivering to be used. Her black veil and gloves were on the floor.

'Ukaleq, please, this place is about to go, everywhere else has been falling for hours.'

'Leave me, Thorne.'

'I will not leave you Ukaleq, you know I cannot leave you. We have been through too much to give in now.'

'I come here every day to speak to him, every single day without fail. Morning, noon and night, and every day he is harder to reach. I think he is telling me to join him now.'

Ser Alderman took a deep breath knowing that Ukaleq was fragile and vulnerable right now, and he had to choose his words sensitively. 'You have been mourning a long time, Ukaleq. Maybe he is saying it is time to let go.'

They both sank back into a previous life, a peaceful life full of promise, where, on a clear day, the island could be seen from the mainland, the long ridge of a tree-fringed hill breaking the horizon to the south. This island was called Saark and long ago they'd been part of a group of travellers who'd settled there. They built their stone dwellings on the top of a hill and planted olive trees for shade. Their buildings had no floors, other than the grass and rock that had been there since the dawn of time. They had no roof, for the dwellers wished to be at one with nature where they could see the sun rise in the east and set in the west, where they could watch the moon change shape in the night sky, and where the seasons could be determined through a difference in the surroundings. They discovered ancient giant monoliths girthed by a circle of smaller standing stones, and here they celebrated an abundance of good fortune.

Though on the mainland, with stories of wizards and witches, of talking beasts and strange underwater phenomena, of supernatural occurrences and para-normal activity, fear was breeding fast.

Ukaleq was married to Augur, a handsome young man in the prime of his youth; strong, resilient, a fair man, an honest man, a man with a quest to instil peace and harmony among all.

But one day, at the onset of dawn, the idyllic tran-quillity of Saark was broken.

The wagons came first, rolling across the fertile land on padded wheels, accompanied by bands of silent raiders. They moved fast, knowing they had very little time to do their vital work. Ahead of them, loping at speed, ran the archers, each man carrying a bow, a quiver of arrows and a bundle of oil-soaked kindling.

There came a shout from the settlement. A shepherd had encountered the raiders. Now others began to wake, and flames began to flicker. But already a greater light was burning in one of the byres, and the breeze was fanning the flames. Another sprang up in a provision shed, and then a third, and within minutes there was a line of fires devouring their peaceful haven. The people ran out, waking to find their settlement ablaze, pouring out of their dwellings, half dressed, confused and frightened.

One of the raiders stepped forward with darting eyes and a booming voice. 'My name is Valdis. You will not be harmed! Do as you are ordered, and you will not be harmed!'

The roaming raiders repeated the cry. 'Remain where you are! You will not be harmed!'

Valdis ordered the wagons to be brought forward. And like a group of snarling beasts, they rumbled into the heart of the crowd. The pall-bearers retreated as Valdis spoke up.

'You are all to come with us. I have been ordered to remove you from this place of evil, for what you are practising here is not how civilised people behave.'

Augur tried to settle his people as he made his way towards Valdis. 'My name is Augur and I am the leader here, and I can tell you that we are doing nothing wrong. You can see that we are simple folk living off the land.' He extended his arm to show the meagre surroundings. 'We choose to live this far away so that we can be left alone to live our lives how we wish.'

'But how you live is not normal. It is not classed as civilised, and what you do is spread fear with your insidious incantations and devil worship.'

Augur laughed. 'We do not worship the devil and we do not spread fear. We are honourable people and live alongside our neighbours without harm. We raise livestock for food and we take from nature what we need.'

'Nonsense,' boomed Valdis. 'I think you find it amusing that people on the mainland are terrified of you. We all know that your rituals and sacrifices and unnatural behaviour is born from devil worship; and today, I am here to stop it.' Valdis nodded once and his men rushed forward and seized Augur by both arms.

Augur tried desperately to struggle free, but the raiders gripped him tighter and threw him into a wagon, the barred door locking behind him with a clang and grinding of bolts. 'If we fall, then you will too. How can humans exist if they can't live alongside each other in peace?'

His words fell on deaf ears.

'Silence! I am your leader now, and my orders will be obeyed.' Valdis looked around and heard the rushing murmur of voices. His words were being repeated all across the settlement. Augur stood at the bars, his hands rattling the impenetrable poles, flared eyes searching for Ukaleq. She ran up to the cage and tried to undo the lock, her small fingers useless against the rigid metal.

'Let him go!' her voice screamed panic. 'He's done nothing wrong.'

'He is a sinner, and sinners need to find their place with the devil. Sinners are not permitted to breathe the same air as those of us who uphold righteousness.'

Valdis gave a sign, and one of his men stepped forward with a burning torch. Beneath the cage was an iron tray, in which lay a deep bed of firewood topped by oil-soaked kindling. Above the kindling, the floor of the cage was an open iron grid. As the kindling caught fire, Ukaleq realised Augur was about to be burned alive. She stepped back as the heat scorched her hands, her arms, her face. It singed the ends of her long hair. She tried to scream but the smoke rendered her mute, she wanted to cry out but even her tears would not run in the poisoned air.

All the raiders were so engrossed in watching a young man burn to death that they didn't notice a cloaked figure put a gloved hand around the woman's mouth and lead her away.

'You will be silent!' commanded Valdis, pacing round the enclosure, immune to the impregnable smoke and cries of pain. 'For each noise you make, I will take another person from you, and they will die in the same way.'

A terrible silence fell over the people of Saark. How could they think of disobeying? Even the bravest of them, even those willing to face death, dared not bring about the death of others. So they made no noise at all as the fire spread in the deep tray, and they closed their eyes to the human sacrifice in front of them.

'People of Saark,' Valdis called to the shocked and silent crowd. 'Your home is destroyed. Your evil ways have come to an end. You now belong to me and will follow the path to righteousness.'

The raiders began pushing the new slaves into the

remaining wagons, unaware that Ukaleq and a saviour had made a daring escape by boat. The last thing Ukaleq saw was the image of her husband being devoured by unforgiving flames. But Augur died in peace, knowing that his best friend had just saved her life.

꒰ ꒰ ꒰

'You saved my life once before, Thorne. I cannot let you do it again. You are going to ask me to leave this place, to leave Augur, and I simply can't do it. I would rather die in here with all my memories than run away again.'

'Do not speak like that, Ukaleq. Remember our talks about life and destiny—the good and the bad, the evil and the triumph. How the good die young and others live a long and prosperous life. We've talked about what happened to Augur and to the others so many times.'

Ukaleq looked up to the ceiling again. 'What would Augur want me to do?'

'He would want you to live, Ukaleq, he would want you to live out the dream that he had for us. He would want us to continue what he started.'

She lifted her head with sadness etched across her

face. 'Why, Thorne? Why? Haven't we been through enough? Watching Augur die at the hands of those men, and having to leave the others to their fate while we ran away.' Her heavy head dropped into her hands as she released the tears.

'He would want you to carry on. He would not want you to give up.'

'But I tried to do that here, Thorne, when we first found this place, I thought that was what Augur wanted for me.'

'It was never ours, Ukaleq. It gave us safety for a long time, but it was never ours. Now we have to go and start another clan, just like Augur wanted.'

'The hunters have destroyed this sacred place, just like the raiders destroyed Saark.'

'Titan had started to weep long before the hunters got here.'

'It knew, didn't it? So why didn't it simply slip away and forego all this death and destruction.'

'Because then people wouldn't have seen their paths. People wouldn't have discarded their old skin and been reborn.'

She reached for his hand. 'Guide me, Thorne, stay with me as I tread this new path.'

He took her hand and kissed it. 'Titan summoned

the Tribunes from the Kingdom of Durundal, so maybe it is telling us to go there.'

'There is a mountain range called The Giant's Claw in Durundal, I have heard the Tribunes talking about it.'

'We will go there and head another community under the protection of The Giant's Claw. We will teach, we will grow and we will learn as part of a clan, just like Augur wanted.'

'And take our people with us?'

'Whoever wishes to join us can follow us. But they won't be called Tribunes and Officials anymore, they will be friends who are striving for the same thing.'

Ukaleq nodded. 'Yes, I agree, that's the way forward now.'

'It will be a long journey, and we will have to find a ship that will take all of us to Durundal. If you remember, the rowing boat that we stole away in only fits a couple of people but we are all still young and strong, so we can make the journey together.'

She looked down at her gems. 'My jewels will be payment. I have no use for them where we will be going.'

'That's more like it. There is always an answer if you look deep enough.'

She felt the exquisite stones between her fingers. 'Another challenge, another journey.'

'It is, Ukaleq, but life is always full of challenges and journeys.'

'I had to hide away for so many years in case someone recognised me. I lived in fear in case we were all rounded up and put in cages of fire. Now, I am not afraid anymore.'

'Not all brave people are soldiers or warriors. Sometimes it takes more courage to face one's fears. Now that you have, you can relinquish your disguise and embrace your freedom.' He held out his hand.

As she got up from the throne and extended her fingers to him, the walls began to shiver and crack, the floor heaved, and chunks of stone crashed to the floor from the ceiling.

'Run, Ukaleq, it's falling apart. I'm right behind you.'

She ran down the aisle, the candles going out as she flew past. The door was ajar, and as she stepped out of the chapel, the ground began to shake, huge mouths of earth gaped hungrily and the complex began to sink slowly into the ground. Another tremulous wave rumbled. Ukaleq put her hands over her ears to drown out the sound. Thorne wrapped his arms around her and ushered her to safety. The trees shook with each monumental movement. It was like a colossal earthquake had hit the epicentre of the world. Trees toppled over easily, while bushes stood like war-torn old sentinels, but the ground slowly consumed them all. The sky was filling with clouds of debris. The lights went out as the chapel went down, and all the other buildings followed.

Finally, with a noise that roared into the sky and sent out tons of dust for several miles around, the giant Titan disappeared, and with it, the history and magic of a time gone by.

Ukaleq was still holding on to Thorne as the grand palace disappeared from view, leaving just a few misplaced stones as evidence of a former existence. She grabbed his hand even tighter.

'I didn't believe it would really happen, Thorne.'

'We protected the giant Titan, and we did well, but with such a force against us, it knew that man still has a lot to learn.'

Ukaleq wiped away a tear and nodded in agreement. 'We have been persecuted once again, and I pray our next destination will be our final one. Though I will miss everything here, literally everything; even the veil and cloak that made me as much of an enigma as Titan itself.'

'You will always be an enigma, Ukaleq, I can promise you that.' He kissed her hand.

❧ ❧ ❧

Ukaleq peered through the brume. The falling dust and debris mottled the sea with spinning rings. It also served as a screen between her and the vessel that had just come into view. She peered at it in disbelief. It was a larger craft, narrow with one sail. The hull was polished wood with a dragon as a figurehead, the tall masts and mainsail were of red and white cloth. Banks of oars rose and fell in unison. 'Can't be!' she exclaimed.

'What is it?' Thorne peered through his spyglass to get a closer look and then he saw more of them—at least twenty ships coming over the horizon. Unlike anything he had seen before, he marvelled at the workmanship as their prows and sterns curled high, tipped with finely crafted dragons. The low sun flashed off the wet blades, and slithers of light were left dancing on the waves. And as the oars disappeared from view, they spooned the tide and came back into view with glistening silver drops running down the paddles. Mesmerised, Thorne continued to observe their course and then he realised the boats were heading for the bay. The guillemots shrieked, the puffins panicked and the Arctic terns flew as high as the masts—for these strange giants were as new to them as they were to him.

As they got nearer, Thorne could see that the boats had twelve oars on each side, manned by twenty-four strong muscular men with long flaxen hair. Another man, who, at over six foot was considerably taller than the rest, held onto the prow with one arm and wielded a sword with the other. He wore a mail shirt and a helmet, his eyes fixed straight ahead as the boat cut through the water like a scythe. Her bow would sometimes break from a wave so the front of her hull, all dark and slimy with growth, would rear skywards with the dragon roaring upwards, and then it would come crashing down with the sea exploding around her sleek hull. With the men groaning and straining with each rotation, the long timber oars fought the waves at every sweep. It was at this point that Ukaleq looked back at Thorne.

'I've had this premonition for months now.'

'Premonition?' Thorne continued to observe the advancing fleet.

'Yes, I saw that more dragons will come to help us, and that's what I thought would happen ... but I didn't realise they would be boats ...I thought they would be beasts.'

'So who are these people?' Thorne faced Ukaleq.

'These are the Vikings that will set up home here.'

'There will be more boats?'

'Most certainly there will be more boats, with more people, a lot more people. There will be battles here for many more years, they will attack places of tranquillity and take what isn't theirs; so we have to leave now if we want to find peace.'

'This is the reason Titan took the dragon city beneath the ground.' Thorne almost whispered the revelation.

Ukaleq shivered. 'Yes, I can see that now, and why we have to leave.'

Thorne's eyes started to widen as he pieced together the final parts of the puzzle. 'Ukaleq, this is our way home, we will 'buy' a couple of boats from the visitors and leave the jewels as payment. We will go tonight, when the visitors are sleeping. We can sail south and be safe under The Giant's Claw in a few days.'

'And the dragons?'

'They will have to go to north and live with the Ice-Dragons. They will be safest there. We already know that the terrain is too harsh for humans.'

'A new start for all of us then?'
'Yes, a new start.'

ga ga ga

The vessels had been moving along at a good speed for many weeks now, and their supplies were incredibly low. Water barrels were nearly empty, and tempers short. Arguably, the oarsmen were the most tired, but all hearts were lifted when the lookout spotted cliffs and caves, and the blisters of rocks made an appearance from the water. This was the first bit of land they had seen in months and they would settle here—permanently.

When they docked, clangour ruled the quay. Men stood on shore unloading casks of wine, sacks of flour, and a trip of indignant goats. The women would have many clothes to mend and several more to wash after so long at sea. The noise was a swelling tide of testosterone, insults and banter. The boats bobbed up and down in the water as they were relieved of their cargo. The children ran off ahead, eager to explore this exciting new land. Chickens and geese stabbed the ground with hungry beaks and ravenous claws. This was their home and history was about to change once again.

CHAPTER TWENTY-EIGHT

A group had gathered around Bard. Zmeitsa was beside him and exposed the fatal wounds to her body. Hydra slithered over to her. 'What can I do, tell me?'

'There is nothing you can do, dear friend, you have done everything you can.'

Hydra looked down at her monstrous form.

'I can still change you, I still have the power.'

'I do not want to be beautiful again, Zmeitsa, just a simple peasant woman will do me. Someone who can live on this bit of land in peace.'

'My powers are waning, so that is probably all I can summon.'

Hydra suddenly felt a wave of emotion pass over her and compassion took over. 'Save yourself,

Zmeitsa, your sons need you. I have grown used to this body now.'

'I wouldn't have my sons if it wasn't for you. The dragons would not have survived if you had not come to our aid.'

'It feels good to do something nice for a change.' Her cackle shook the ground and everything around it.

'I made a promise to you, and from today you shall be known as Aquila. Aquila the Seer, the bird woman, the oracle who knows everything.'

Hydra smiled contentedly, all of her eyes closed in anticipation, her body braced for the transformation, and with a nod of her head Zmeitsa summoned Sagitta over.

'Torch her.'

Sagitta looked horrified and everyone looked on aghast. The Grandmaster held her hands to her mouth.

'Do it, do it now!' screamed Zmeitsa.

'You promised me. Zmeitsa, you gave me your word.'

'Hurry, Sagitta, we don't have much time.'

Sagitta summoned all his energy and sent a ball of fire over Hydra. Zmeitsa joined him with the little energy she had left. The flames turned Hydra blacker than before, as she screamed and cursed trying to escape the blaze. Her limbs were flailing, the stench was overpowering. The monster rose and fought back trying to escape the tongues of death.

'Do not stop, Sagitta, we have to kill her.'

He circled like a predator, breathing his flames over her body. Even though every part of his being was telling him to stop, he could not go against his mother.

The heads were trying to find a way out of the flames; screaming, snapping, snarling, the jaws of hell opened wider than ever before and the rows of teeth melted as Sagitta continued to send balls of fire over her. The creature stood no chance; without the water to protect her, she sank to the floor and pitifully beat at the soil.

'You can stop now, Sagitta, our job is done.'

Sagitta hung his head in shame. The onlookers were visibly shaken, some wanted to scream at Zmeitsa, most looked for Ser Alderman to help, for all of them would have perished without Hydra.

But then a strange thing happened. The flames grew taller again and the ashes lifted in a frenzy and swirled around the body at such a rate it was impossible to watch. Everyone turned their heads from the vision and used their hands as shields. Round and round it went, again and again and again, then it stopped as abruptly as it had begun. Left behind was something on the floor. A body of some description, but what was it? The being stood up from the ashes; long grey hair covered its body, an elderly woman turned around and bright blue eyes looked at the world from a different perspective for the first time in two hundred years. She looked at her hands, she felt her face, she ran her fingers through her hair. She smiled for the first time and then laughed out loud as she embraced her nakedness.

Ukaleq ran forward and wrapped her cloak around Aquila. 'I do not wish to cover you up for you are such a beautiful woman, but the stars are too far away to keep you warm, and I do not want you to catch a chill.'

'And as I am reborn, so too are you, Ukaleq, it is good to see you without your disguise.'

Ukaleq nodded her head and kissed Aquila's hand.

'We have all been transformed this night,' said Zmeitsa, stepping forward in human form. 'I couldn't explain earlier, for I didn't know how much time I had left.'

They all looked over at Sagitta who was still breathing out smoke. But his red scales had turned green. He was an adult now and as his mother became human again, he stood over Bard in a protective stance, and Bellatrix leaned into him with pride.

'My son, my warrior, my dearest Sagitta, what a fine dragon you have become, and I am sorry to have concerned you so when you torched Aquila, but know that she will be forever in your debt.' She sensed his love for all three women. 'This night you must leave Bard and take Bellatrix to Boreas Crown in the mountains. You will be safe with the Ice-Dragons, all of you will be safe. And I can tell you, from a very reliable source, that the interior is on a par with the Dragon Palace of Bergen.'

Sagitta leaned in to Bellatrix and a plume of smoke came through his nostrils.

'Please take care of Lepus for me, ' continued the Mother. 'She has been instrumental in this triumphant win, and saved a lot of lives.'

Of course I will, came the transmitted thought.

Lepus nuzzled the Mother. *I will miss you, Zmeitsa. You have taught me everything.*

And I will miss you, Lepus, my little hare. You have come a long way; you have learned so much. And be sure to spread the silver on the journey, after such a battle, most will need it. Lepus nuzzled her. *I made sure I brought enough.*

I knew you would. The hare sees everything. But look,

the dragons are coming over to thank you and welcome you into the family.

The Mother watched as Antares, the stag, was the first to greet Lepus by way of an embrace, and then the other dragons followed. Her work here was nearly done, she just had one more thing to do, and went over to the transformed women.

Aquila held out her hands. 'You died during the process didn't you?'

'I did, and it was very peaceful, I was in no pain,' Zmeitsa replied.

'I'm glad, and thank you for giving up your life so that I might live.'

Zmeitsa smiled at the woman standing before her. 'It was an honour, Aquila, and I'm sorry again to have alarmed you as I did—but I do need you to do one more thing for me.'

'Anything, Zmeitsa.'

'Bard will wake up later and I will have gone. Everyone will have gone except you and him. He will forget everything about his former life with me. That is the prophecy should I die. But I want you to take my place as his mother. Tell him you found him as a little boy of four and how he played with his brother in the ruins over there. Tell him that he has to join forces with the Vikings now—for that is his destiny. Please ensure he does this.'

Aquila felt the emotion rise up. 'I am to become a mother. I am going to have a family. Thank you, Zmeitsa, thank you.'

'You have earned that right, my dearest friend, and just like Ukaleq will have many followers, Bard is now your ward.'

'I will be more than happy to do that for you, Zmeitsa, of course I will. But what about his time here, will he forget that as well?'

'Not all of it. His weapon training will remain as part of his ancestral knowledge, he will remember Sagitta, but everything else will be a vague memory. To him, his life has been with you. Though tell him stories of his conception, he will find that particularly fascinating—one day.'

'I will do everything you have asked of me, Zmeitsa.'

'Take this necklace as a sign of my gratitude. It is the star of Aquila, the eagle in the night sky. You can spread your wings now and guide my two son's as they find their place in the kingdoms.'

Aquila slipped the necklace over her head and let it rest against the cloak. 'I may have saved your sons, but *you* have saved me and given me a new life.'

'Fate is like that, you just never know what is around the corner. Only the constellations stay the same; the only path you can be sure of in life.'

'Where will you go now?' asked Ukaleq.

'I must return to The Cave of Secrets, the sisters are waiting for me there.' Zmeitsa looked at Ukaleq and held out her hands. 'You are a great healer with an ability to see things before they happen. I can see your path is full of guidance and leadership as you set up home under The Giant's Claw. It's what Augur would have wanted. It's what he has always wanted for you.'

'Thorne said the very same thing.' Ukaleq looked back at him with affection and wiped away the tear.

'He is right, Ukaleq. You have great powers. And do not despair that Titan sits below the ground now. The dragon city will rise again one day. Even the underwater city where Hydra once lived, will rise again when mankind has become as great as the old ones; understanding of acceptance and beyond all evil.'

'That may be a long time coming, Zmeitsa. People are arriving who will bring more misery to the lives of others. But I do know that we learn from each generation and it's the only way we will live like the 'old ones' again.'

'I am hopeful of a better future,' said Zmeitsa, and then she furrowed her brow in deeper thought. 'I can also see that Thorne has a pivotal role to fulfil, and though he doesn't know it, and neither do you, I can tell you that the stag and the hare are the bearers of a new dawn.'

'I will remember that Zmeitsa. Thank you. Perhaps the giant Titan planned this all along; to expose each of us in our true form and guide us towards our path.' Ukaleq stepped forward to hug the Mother.

'I believe so,' said Zmeitsa returning the embrace.

Aquila nodded in agreement. 'My destiny is to remain here. I will remain close to my past domain, and witness it rising when the time is right. Plus, as I am now the proud mother of a special young man called Bard, I will be close by whenever he needs me.'

The women held hands tightly and then embraced.

But Zmeitsa had begun to fade away and the two women watched as her image disappeared into a speck on the horizon.

Bard murmured as his mother disappeared. Sagitta reached down to nuzzle him with his huge snout, but Bard was still in a deep sleep.

'I spoke with him once,' said Ukaleq, aware that Bard's injuries had healed completely. All of the burned skin had sloughed away, and the deep laceration had been replaced with healthy pink flesh. She smiled as she recalled that particular morning. 'It was his birthday, and it was only by chance that we spoke. When I asked how he knew it was his birthday he told me that his mother had taught him to observe the position of the sun and the stars in the sky.' Ukaleq smiled in reverie. 'I saw something very special in him that day. I requested that he fight with the Fellow of Swords in the arena, and that's when I saw his deep ancestral knowledge.'

'Yes, he is indeed very special,' said Aquila. 'Like his mother and his brother, they all have special gifts.'

Ukaleq let out a big sigh at what might have been, remembering how fate had changed her own path. 'I have to summon the people together and explain what we have to do now. I have never done that before. Ser Alderman always spoke for me.'

'This is *your* destiny. This is *your* path. Gather your people and speak to them from your heart. They *will* follow you.' Aquila smiled at Ukaleq and nodded serenely as she watched her gather everyone around.

The people hadn't really noticed this stranger in their midst. So many distractions and paranormal events had been occurring, another woman stepping out of the shadows seemed to be a natural happening. But when this stranger, who had but seconds ago been in talks with the Mother and Aquila, started to gather everyone around, muttering ensued.

'People of the Dragon Palace in Bergen, people of the lowlands, people who have fought and defeated an army. I salute you. I salute your bravery, your comradeship, your fearlessness. And I applaud my dearest ally.' She looked at Aquila and with both hands on her heart, dipped her head in respect.

'Today, I stand before you, with a voice, a heart and the body of a woman.' There were cheers and shouts as she acknowledged their collective reception. 'But, it is not as a woman descended from noble ancestry that I speak, nor as a woman that has powers from beyond the grave, but as a woman who seeks to be seen and heard and touched. I am the Grandmaster who, for so many years hid behind a veil, covered from head to toe in a cloak, with my hands and arms hidden from view within gloves. I was wrong when I thought I had to hide myself away. I was wrong to be scared. I was wrong to think I had a terrible secret. As a good friend of mine recently told me, Not all brave people are soldiers or warriors.' She sought out Thorne in the crowd and acknowledged him among the raucous applause, cries of unity and whistles of pride. She called for calm by raising the palm of her hand. 'Today is a new day, and I stand before you as a woman. And like Aquila, and Zmeitsa, I am a woman who wishes to be recognised.' There were more cheers and roars of support as she took another deep breath. 'Today will bring new beginnings for us all.' She sought Aquila and Thorne in the crowd and nodded. 'Today's events have caused us to reconsider our options. Titan is at peace now and has taken the great Dragon Palace with it, so we too must go to pastures new.' She waited for the murmurs to recede. 'We will be leaving here very soon and sail to Durundal. Our dragons will go to Boreas Crown and live in peace with the mighty Ice Dragons in the mountains; so say your goodbyes for they will have to leave soon. We will take a few of the boats that have recently arrived on our shores—and know that my jewels will be left as payment. Those who wish to return to their homes and their families will be given safe passage. Those who wish to remain with Ser Alderman and myself will be welcomed as we establish a new settlement which we will call the Clan of The Giant's Claw. From this moment on I will be known as Ukaleq. There will be no more Fellows, Guardians, Heralds, Readers, Temple Boys and Tribunes, denoted in rank by a colour. We are as one and will be known by first names only. That means Ser Alderman will be known as Thorne, and he will be the leader he has always been.' She acknowledged Thorne as he stood with Aquila. 'We will leave this place now. The only one who will know its history will be Aquila—for it is her destiny to remain with the secrets of the Dragon Palace. We wish her well. We wish Bard well, and we wish the dragons well. My people, gather your belongings and follow us to a new beginning.'

There was rapturous applause as Thorne escorted her from the podium and they bid their farewells to the mighty dragons who had served them all so well. Mensa, Lupus, Pardalis, Antares, Noctua, Sagitta, Bellatrix and Lepus.

The former Officials, including, Fellow 135, Alto, Sli, Saul, Ramou and Dom acknowledged Bard for his bravery and comradeship, and followed Ukaleq and Thorne to the boats.

Sagitta carried Bard to his new accommodation, a small dwelling overlooking the sea that Aquila had chosen, close enough to the ruins, yet far enough away from the new Viking settlement. He laid him down on the ground carefully and tried to use his telepathy, but it had gone. He nuzzled his brother, but the young man stayed asleep. He wanted Bard to see his brand new scales, to see that he was an adult now and that Sagitta and Bellatrix were finally united. A stray tear fell on Bard's lips. That tear would heal any wound, but more importantly, it would hold their bond in Bard's subconscious mind.

Bard had changed as well and was about to embark

on a new life with the Vikings. Sagitta saw the constellations above and watched as the dragons drifted beneath them. Their lasting image was the ruins of a time gone by, and the dragon pool which had been left intact as a symbol of the past. With one last look at his brother and a nod of acceptance from Aquila, he stood tall, stretched his new green wings and took to the skies with Bellatrix at his side.

They were heading towards a twilight kingdom where daylight would last for little more than three hours, and before they reached their journey's end they would be travelling through perpetual night. Here, the temperatures would tumble even further and a thick rime of ice would cover everything. The wind would carve the snow into fantastic sculptures, and icicles would hang perilously from contorted shapes. Home would be a magnificent natural phenomenon that climbed into majestic spires and turrets and towers, white and glistening against the frozen landscape. Here, the true magic of nature would keep the hunters away; for the air burns with a piercing cold that can freeze human skin within seconds, and turns human eyeballs to ice in less than that. The lungs turn to stone and the breath congeals on impact.

An abundance of animals had been forced to adapt

to these harsh conditions, for they would rather take their chances with the dragons than be hunted to extinction by the humans.

With a complex underground system of heated thermal currents, spring-fed pools and cavernous chambers threaded with silver, the dragons would, at last, be safe, and here they will live in peace, with the Ice Dragons of Boreas Crown.

EPILOGUE

Bard was dreaming: He was in a castle and he sat up slowly as a nauseating sound of death filtered into his room.

'We have to go now.' It was his mother, asking him to do the very thing that he feared the most.

In his dream, he whispered a frail response in disbelief. 'Why?'

'We are in danger, the castle is under siege and we must go to the tunnel. I will be with you all the way, I promise. I will be right behind you. It's safe in there. Nothing will hurt you. But we must make haste.' The instructions became more hurried.

'Mother, I can't. I would rather die here than go in there.' His voice was thick with fear now. The smoke had reached them and the castle was falling in around them.

'My sweet son, I would do anything to spare you this, but you have to be brave, we all have to be so very brave.'

The flashing lights of fire and the constant stream of wailing terrified him. If he wanted to live then he had to go through the tunnel with his mother, and he knew that he didn't want to die. His mother wrapped a shawl around him and guided him out of his room.

The air was claustrophobic with smoke, and shallow pools of debris littered the way like old, abandoned toys. His mother picked her way through them as carefully as she could, avoiding the six-foot-long nails that protruded like hideous flags of honour, and blocks of black basalt so large that they must have taken a hundred men to hoist them into place. The main tower collapsed behind them, and as they ran through the broken masonry, she yelled out all the instructions that would see him to safety—but the gnarled fingers of death grabbed her words before they reached his ears.

Outside, there still raged screams and crying, running footsteps, the whinny of petrified dragons and the frantic barking of terrified dogs. They were now at the concealed entrance. The door was heavy and already had piles of asphalt blocking its access. She couldn't open it on her own. Despite everything in his head telling him not to, Bard dropped to his knees and pawed at the fallen masonry with his bare hands.

As it edged open her stricken voice ushered him in. 'Go ahead of me. I will be right behind you. Remember everything I have told you, keep going to the end, don't turn back, just run as fast as you can.'

But a figure had entered the room and loomed over him like a grim reaper against the black smoke. The figure grabbed Bard, pulled his head back with one hand, and held a knife to his throat with the other. The scream stuck in his mother's throat; she had seconds to do something before the blade penetrated her son's neck. Bard had his trembling hands on the man's arms, his eyes frantic, voice disabled, body writhing like an eel to get free. He kicked back at his attacker with his bare feet, but the man merely laughed and tightened his grip.

'No, please no,' his mother cried, but only a whisper escaped.

The fiend bore into her eyes with a vicious stare, and began to slowly pierce her son's skin.

'No!' she screamed out loud and grabbed a piece of granite from the ground and hurled it against the hunter's head. A trickle of blood ran down from his temple. Bard was thrown to the floor as the brute turned his attention to his mother.

'Go! Go now!' she screamed.

He could hear her voice urging him to follow the path, so he walked a bit faster and then a bit more until the dark was rushing towards him. Deeper into the shrinking cavern he went, grazing his flying arms on the ridges of molten rock, tearing the soles of his feet on the uneven surface, but her voice told him to keep going. On and on he went, for miles it seemed, he didn't know how far. There was little air in the passage and soon he felt his lungs burning. It was cold and damp, and his heart was pounding but still he ran.

Beads of fear ran down his back in rivulets, and he knew that he must have covered a fair distance when the breath caught in his throat and he found it hard to breathe. He slowed to a trot but his tired limbs couldn't steady his balance. Tripping over misplaced legs he stumbled and fell, his hands and buttocks landing straight in a mud pool.

'Get up, Bard, keep going, your life depends on it.'

The emerging bruise on his thigh went unnoticed as he slowly hauled himself up and staggered some hundred yards—but his legs were useless now. Torn, gashed, and weary, he could run no more. His heart was pounding and the only thing he could see was the silvery vapour of his own breath. 'I have to be...' His back found a crevasse in his damp dark surroundings. 'Brave.' As his voice trailed off, he pulled his knees tight against his chest and tried to sleep.

A gentle breeze brushed his face and shone a light to the outside world. His weary eyes opened to find that his crevasse was the mouth of a cave, and outside hung grey skies and a hazy sun. He felt his gashed neck and winced. New bruises ached, and his wounds began to sting as he stretched out his entwined limbs and crawled slowly to the entrance of his tomb.

He looked fearfully out of the small opening. Spots danced dizzily before his eyes as they adjusted to the light, but when they did, a grass-covered expanse of land loomed and the sound of running water sent spasms to his parched mouth. And in the mist he noticed something. A figure. It was his mother holding her arms out to him. Her voice was calling him.

'Are you all right, Bard? Bard, are you okay?'

Bard awoke with a start. He smiled when he saw the familiar face of his mother.

Aquila brushed the hair from his face. 'You were thrashing about a lot.'

He sat up and wiped the sleep from his gritty eyes. 'I've just had the strangest dream. I was in a tunnel running away from something, but I couldn't run. It was dark, cold, and scary but at the end of the tunnel was a new destination, a different place... and you were there to greet me.'

'Perhaps it means something, Bard. Dreams tend to convey messages. But up you get, I've done your breakfast. I know that you like to eat early.'

'Thank you, Mother.'

Aquila smiled when she called her that, no one had ever called her *Mother* before, but she suddenly stopped in mid-thought. 'Oh, I nearly forgot. We had new arrivals in the night. Maybe you'd like to go and introduce yourself.'

'Really?'

'Yes, really, I think you will find some new friends there.'

'All right, I will go and take a look later on today when I've finished my chores.'

'Good lad; so maybe your dream is about change.'

'I think it is, and I could do with some excitement in my life.'

They both smiled—but Aquila smiled the longest.

There are none who can say with certain knowledge when the Kingdom of Durundal began, yet this has not stopped the dragons, the kings, the sorcerers and other wise-ones from seeking the answer. What we do know is that the dragons ruled supreme and considered by many to be the dawn of time.

Since the dragons started to disappear, man has ruled the earth. Barbaric, uncivilised, numerous—most with a hunger for wealth, many corrupted by power. We know this because of untold riches discovered in burial sites, and stories that have been passed down since the dawn of time. Henceforth, I bring you my vision of The Kingdom of Durundal. Set in the turbulent age of this ancient world, my eleven-book series follows the clashes between the clans and the courts amid the tumultuous struggles for power.

During this time, no monarch was more feared than Emperor Gnaeus III of Ataxata, along with his general, Domitrius Corbulo, and much later his heir, Cornelius, whose cruelty to Namir (King of the Clans) had become legendary throughout the Kingdom of Durundal. Each of those tyrants had a tale of tragedy, a moment in history that changed them from righteous and ardent to nefarious and malevolent; each wretched memory a painful reminder of what might have been.

It is said that the deceased warriors, tribunes and dragons who fought so bravely to protect Titan in those early days, still live beneath the ruins; and even today it is forbidden to enter the sacred monument, guarded at all times by the presence of Aquila.

The Kingdom of Durundal is a complex place, and the books are written in such a way that the characters' lives interconnect, and what happens at the very end of book eleven, sets the scene for book one. The series is an ongoing cycle that can be read again and again for the reader to uncover more connections, more family history, and more hidden meanings. With elements of fantasy, history, and ancient mythology, immerse yourself in this epic adventure.

I have enjoyed creating this multi genre series and crafting the characters and their journeys as well as researching the many topics that bring this series to life. I now look forward to reading your reviews and how my characters' lives have touched your own.

The Dragon Palace in Bergen. All the dragons are named after stars.

Bellatrix—Female Warrior

Mensa—The Mountain

Sagitta—The Arrow

Pardalis—The Leopard

Pavo—The Peacock

Noctua—The Moth

Antares—The Stag

Lacerta—The Lizard

Lupus—The Wolf

Pyxis—The Compass

Aquila—The seer and wise woman—means Eagle

Castle Dru in Durundal—all dragons apart from Zmeitsa are named after stars.

Zmeitsa—is a female dragon that seduces men to spawn offspring in dragon and human form. (Zmeitsa in the Kingdom of Durundal series seduces Cornelius of Ataxata and Segan Hezekiah.)

Cygnus—Swan

Lyra—Harp

Vega—Falling Eagle
Delphinus—Dolphin
Lepus—Hare

The plaques on the walls of the Grandmaster's private chapel, depict images of a hare, a wolf, a leopard, a stag, and a moth.

These are the dragons that survive alongside Sagitta and Bellatrix, and Mensa—the mother.

Lepus—the hare
Lupus—the wolf
Pardalis—the leopard
Antares—the stag
Noctua—the moth

The images on the other side of the wall represent the five stages of woman.

The Maiden
The Mother
The Crone
The Goddess
Rebirth

Ukaleq and **Thorne** can be found in *A Hare in the Wilderness,* Ajeya's first refuge in the Clan of The Giant's Claw, they are also in *A Stag in the Shadows.*

Aquila is pivotal in *SEVERN* and *SABLE.*

Cornelius (father of Sansara)—*A Leopard in the Mist, A Stag in the Shadows, A Moth in the Flames, Sorceress of the Sapphire part one.*

Segan Hezekiah (father of Bard and Sagitta) can be found in *A Stag in the Shadows* and *A Moth in the Flames.*

Sansara is Zmeitsa's daughter with Cornelius and can be found in *A Moth in the Flames* and *Sorceress of the Sapphire parts 1 and 2*

The Goddess of the Temple and **Keeper of Dragons** can be found in *Sorceress of the Sapphire part 3*

The epilogue is taken from *A Wolf in the Dark* as Lyall (from Castle Dru in Durundal) mirrors Bard's transition from boy to man as he enters a different world through a disused tunnel.

The line that Zmeitsa speaks:

'You are right, Lepus. But the hare has to find the stag, and wars have to be fought and won; and only when the sorceress of the sapphire becomes the goddess of the temple, will the guiding light shine for the dragons to return.'

The Hare is Ajeya from *A Hare in the Wilderness (Book 1)*

The Stag is Dainn from *A Hare in the Wilderness (Book 1)* Dainn is Thorne's son.

The Goddess of the Temple is Azura (Ajeya and Dainn's granddaughter) from book 8—*Sorceress of the Sapphire part 3,* the final book in the series that precedes the three prequels.

Boreas—God of the North and Winter.

The Tribunes all come from the *Kingdom of Durundal,* and the significant places where they all originate from feature in *A Stag in the Shadows:*

Ramou—Condor Vale

Bard—Castle Dru

Saul—River Dru

Dram—Aiden Hall

Sli—Sturt Manor

Davio—Ataxata

Ijja—East Coast

Alto—Ataxata

Haynes—East Coast

Dom—East Coast

What's Next?

The final book will be a compendium of all the books in the Kingdom of Durundal series. With colour illustrations and decorative text, this will focus on the many themes and subjects explored over the eleven books. It will be called **The Book of Knowledge** which features heavily throughout the series.

And after listening to many requests from all over the world, Audio Books in the complete series will be next to follow.

Listen to podcasts and interviews at: https:// linktr.ee/S.E.Turner

S.E. Turner was born in the UK and currently lives forty miles south of London. Please follow her on Goodreads, BookBub and Instagram, and if you enjoyed the series, please leave a favourable review.

What inspired you to write The Kingdom of Durundal?

A visit to Scotland first inspired me. I found the wilderness to be breathtaking, the vast mountain ranges spectacular, and with its eerie atmosphere, you can almost hear the ancient clans whispering on the horizon. I climbed the great mound of Dunadd Fort in Kilmartin Glen; a royal power to the first Gaelic kings and home to a fortress some 2,000 years ago. From that vantage point, I saw the far-reaching views of the lochs, of castles, of caves and hidden grottos. I saw a story unfold before me. I saw pain and sorrow, love and comradeship, fear and courage. I saw the magic of a time gone by. I saw the Kingdom of Durundal.

As with all kingdoms where clans and courts live side by side; the realms of sacrifice and avarice are prevalent. That is the backbone of my series. Certainly from Book 2 onwards, the true depths to which those in power will go is explored at some length.

Interestingly, from the first moment that Ajeya comes riding in (*A Hare in the Wilderness*), to the part where Sansara returns to Tarragon Island (*A Moth in the Flames*), the timescale is only a few days. It's the history of the main characters that goes back some twenty-five years and it's that connection that holds the story together. *The Sorceress of the Sapphire* continues the family saga and introduces the third and fourth generations—and the final character in Book 8 is Azura, Ajeya's granddaughter. Though, as is usual with folklore and ancient mythology, there has to be magic and dragons—hence the themes and characters in all of the books. Books 9, 10, and 11 are prequels, and introduce the reader to the dawn of the Kingdom of Durundal.

How did you decide on the titles for your books?

When you write about ancient civilisations, albeit in a fantasy setting, there has to be a certain amount of research to keep it believable. Most of what you read about the clans is factual, and their totems are indeed very real. Our ancestors depended on them for safety, to please the spirits, and to give the bearer added strength. I have tried to keep this bygone age alive in my books. The titles in the first four books of the series are the characters totems.

Your female protagonists are very strong. Why did you write them in?

Throughout history, there have been so many inspirational women, women of courage with a fire about them. I want to give all women a platform so that women from all walks of life, women of every colour and creed, women of all ages, will find that inspiration, seek out that courage, and ignite that fire within them.

Think like Cleopatra, fight like Boadicea and live like a goddess.

Who is your favourite character?

I am asked that a lot, and I would have to say Cornelius. I think he had a bad start in life. He was the ultimate bad guy and did some pretty awful stuff to Namir in *A Leopard in the Mist*. He was a liar and a coward. But was it nature or nurture that made him that way? Whatever made him change, he came good in the end (*A Stag in the Shadows*). At that point, I didn't know whether to kill him off or save him. I spent months considering the options. But in the end, I decided to save him, because he is my favourite character. And to show that people can change—if they want to.

What would you say to a fledgling author?

Never give up on your dream. Read a lot of books in different genres, and write down all those little pockets of inspiration that pop into your head at the unlikeliest of moments.

S.E. Turner is a lifelong enthusiast of epic fantasy that borders on the believable. With an abundance of historical research woven through the pages—the Kingdom of Durundal guarantees to be an engaging and immersive experience.

'The series promises to be far more than the single genre of fantasy for one particular audience. Rather, it blends into a

numinous crossroads where fantasy meets reality, and the surreal meets the sublime. I wanted to write a series that everyone could read, and I'm happy to provide an exciting, epic story, that a wide variety of ages will enjoy.'

'In the wrong hands, power is a deadly poison.'